DEADLY INTENTIONS

"Please save us," the two Sioux girls begged. "They make us do awful things here."

"Try anything you can to avoid what the owners wants. In a matter of days I will come back and you will be free."

With those parting words, Rebecca Caldwell opened the door. Another door opened and a mean, middle-aged man stepped out.

"Sa-ay, li'l gal. I didn't see you earlier. You're just the thing I need to finish off the night."

"I don't work here," the White Squaw replied.

"If you don't work here, what are you doin' up here?" Fuzzily, the customer began to suspect something was not quite right.

Before his whiskey- and sex-befuddled brain could react to this suspicion, Rebecca reached into her reticule and brought out her .38 Baby Russian revolver. The nickel plating of the Smith and Wesson glittered in the yellow light of the shaded hall lamps. With a sure, solid movement, she shoved it against the side of his head.

"You and I are going to walk quietly down this hall, down the stairs and out the back like old, dear friends. If anyone stops us, you die first. Is that clear?"

"Y-you really mean that, don't you?" he asked.

"I learned young, mister, never pull a gun on someone unless you have every intention of using it!"

WHITE SQUAW
Zebra's Adult Western Series
by E. J. Hunter

Available wherever paperbacks are sold, or order direct from the Publisher. Send cover price plus 50¢ per copy for mailing and handling to Zebra Books, Dept. 2315, 475 Park Avenue South, New York, N.Y. 10016. Residents of New York, New Jersey and Pennsylvania must include sales tax. DO NOT SEND CASH.

#16

REDSKIN ROSEBUD
—— BY E.J. HUNTER ——

ZEBRA BOOKS
KENSINGTON PUBLISHING CORP.

Special aknowledgements to Mark K. Roberts for his creative contribution to this work.

ZEBRA BOOKS

are published by

Kensington Publishing Corp.
475 Park Avenue South
New York, NY 10016

First printing: March 1988

Printed in the United States of America

This volume of the adventures of Rebecca Caldwell Ridgeway is dedicated with respect and admiration to *Barbara Ketchem*, who sure knows how to put together one helluva convention. See you in '88!

—EJH

"Few of the captive women we recovered wished to be reunited with the finer aspects of civilization. Forced into unbelievable degradation, many preferred to remain with their Indian husbands, rather than face the good people of the white world. Others, may they be forgiven, chose suicide."

—Gen. George Crook
Dispatches

Chapter 1

Age-worn, rounded hills rose in clusters from the surrounding flatlands. Deep gullied ridges spread in places like the fingers of a mammoth hand. Dotted with wage, cacti and stunted pines, they broke up the undulating sameness of the smooth, green prairie that stretched eastward. Hidden in unexpected folds, small streams criss-crossed the vast expanse. It looked much the same everywhere, or so the white man saw it.

"Unbounded sameness," some traveler had once described Dakota Territory, "relieved only by vast areas of unbounded sameness."

To the young woman seated on a large, erosion-smoothed boulder, such a departure from reality held no meaning. It *was* different. Every rock, rill, ridge and valley of the Rosebud Agency differed markedly from the familiar plains and cove-like valleys of home. Although only a half-blood, Rebecca Caldwell Ridgeway felt the loss of that intimate domain with only slightly less sorrow than her personal tragedy.

A widow for only seven months, Rebecca had witnessed the savage murder of her husband and a dearly-loved step-child, before personally avenging

7

both. The killer had been a white man, her uncle, Ezekial Caldwell. Rebecca, and a surviving stepson, Joey Ridgeway, had moved to the village of the Red Top Lodge Oglala Sioux, who had formerly been led by her father, Iron Calf. Their stay in familiar and soothing environs proved a short one.

Due to the exigencies of maintaining a reliable food supply and the constant encroachment of white settlers, and Red Top Oglala had been forced to bow to the inevitable and move onto one of the reservations. Their present civil chief and his council chose the Rosebud Agency. Rebecca now sought solace for her numbing grief among unfamiliar scenes. On the contrary, Joey had adapted much more readily.

He and his new friends, Rebecca reflected a moment, were probably off playing those violent games so devoutly pursued by growing boys. Perhaps the *yugmi oyicayuspapi na, cankpe un poge nawicazuzu po*, the attack-upset-smash-smash-nose, kick-and-swing game. It resulted in lots of bruises, black eyes, bloody noses and occasional broken bone. And the gangly young males of the Oglala band dearly loved it. No matter the injuries, Joey would be right in the middle of it. Rebecca sighed and directed her contemplations onto how to fill the empty hours that stretched day-by-day into her future.

"You did not!"
"I did too!"
"Did not!" Shaking with anger, from his small, moccasin clad feet, through his slender, bronze body to the short braids of white straw hair, *Mahtolasan,*

once called Tommy Archer, shook a hard, bony fist in the face of his adversary.

A ring of coppery brown, black-haired Oglala boys surrounded the disputing pair, each loudly cheering on their champion. The youngsters, ranging in age from ten to thirteen, had been engaged in a rough-and-tumble sort of ball game in which kicking, punching, spitting and biting were permitted to prevent the opposite side from crossing the defender's goal and scoring a point. White Bear Cub had been defending the Blue Feather goal and claimed he prevented *Pinspinzala* from scoring.

Short, stocky, hard muscles rippling under his golden skin, Little Prairie Dog hotly disputed that contention. Gray-brown dust made flat splotches on the sweat-filmed arms, legs and bare torsos of the players. They bubbled with excitement as *Mahtolasan* emphasized his position with a hard shove.

Small fists balled, *Pinspinzala* punched him in the face. With an unconscious gesture, Little Prairie Dog brushed a thick shock of hair, equally as white as *Mahtolasan*'s, out of his eyes and prepared to give further battle. His pugnacious stance was more familiar to his life as Joey Ridgeway, than the newest addition to the Red Top band.

"I said I scored," Joey stated flatly. "You didn't throw me back until I'd crossed the line."

"I got you three paces in front of the line," Tommy insisted.

"Bullshit," Joey snapped, reverting for the first time to English. Then, for emphasis, he added the Oglala equivalent, *"Unkce-pte."*

Mahtolasan had been trying to bully the young

9

orphan since his arrival. Jealousy and the insecurity of the boy Tommy Archer lay behind it. Tommy had been treated with somewhat a state of awe by his contemporaries when he had been adopted into the band. His ability to fight, to learn the language, and to tan as darkly as any Oglala, yet his hair remain white as that of the sacred buffalo, had earned him a special place. Now came this usurper, with the same qualities, to detract a bit from the glory of being White Bear Cub. *Mahtolasan* came at *Pinspinzala* with both arms windmilling.

His blows stung against Joey's skin, yet the youngster paid them no notice. He gave a step, set himself and delivered a solid punch to the center of *Mahtolasan*'s chest. He followed with a left-right-left to the head. *Mahtolasan* stopped moving for a long moment, blinked his eyes and sighed lightly. Abruptly he sat down. *Pinspinzala* dove on top of him and they began to roll about. Shrill hoots of encouragement came from the onlookers.

Mahtolasan wedged an elbow free and cracked a short, hard right on his opponent's face, which set *Pinspinzala*'s nose to bleeding. Joey reared back, ignoring the crimson flow, and began to pummel *Mahtolasan* with fast, stinging jabs. Belly muscles tightened and *Mahtolasan* lurched his pelvis. The movement dislodged *Pinspinzala*, who sprawled a moment in the dirt before jumping upright.

"Had enough?" *Pinspinzala* taunted.

"Naw," *Mahtolasan* panted. "I can whip you."

"Unh-unh. You wanna see?" *Pinspinzala* gasped back.

Snake-quick, he struck again, thin, long-muscled

arms like pistons. *Mahtolasan* grunted and gave ground. His vision wavered. His ears rang. He wanted to cry but damned well wouldn't. One of the Oglala boys stretched out a leg and tripped him from behind. The others giggled, considering it the height of hilarity. *Pinspinzala* dove on top of him. The air exploded from his lungs.

Gasping, he whispered in English. "Joey. Joey, this is stupid."

"Uh, yeah, I know, Tommy." *Pinspinzala* replied in the same language. "We—we oughtta be friends."

"I, ah, know. Lemmie up an' we'll shake on it, okay?"

"You gotta 'give,' first," *Pinspinzala* ordered.

"Awh, shit. Do I?" *Mahtolasan* complained.

"Say, 'give,' or I'll knock you a good one," *Pinspinzala* said unrelentingly.

Tommy Archer took a deep breath, sighed and bellowed, "Enough! I give, I give!"

Joey Ridgeway came to his feet and offered his white brother a hand. A certain look of respect and affection passed between them. Then, together, *Mahtolasan* and *Pinspinzala* turned to face their companions.

"He is brave," *Mahtolasan* stated simply.

"He is a tough fighter," *Pinspinzala* acknowledged.

Hoka, Joey's special friend, came forward and, stepping between them, laid an arm on each one's shoulder. "Together, no one can beat them."

"You're a good friend, *Hoka*," *Pinspinzala* remarked. He still had trouble with the *k'h* sound of the first letter of his friend's name.

"Let's play," Gray Tail grumbled. "What did we

come out here for?"

Laughing and pummeling each other, the boys resumed their game.

Rebecca's reflections had developed into a mental wrestling match. *What's the matter with you,* a part of her conscious attitude revealed, *is that you've got no man in your life.* Since her return to her Oglala people, there had been plenty of suitors, or would-be hopefuls. She had uniformly spurned them all. The way part of her felt, she didn't want one. Not now or ever again. She had been hurt too many times. All of the men she had allowed herself to truly love had been taken from her by violence.

So what? the taunt came back. *You are too young and healthy and your body demands, it must have, tenderness and release. Don't you remember the way Four Horns made love? Or the magical way Bobby Rhodes could thrill you? Or Grover? What if he is gone now?* Grover Ridgeway had been a masterful lover.

"Only too true," Rebecca said aloud. Meaning, her bitter self declared, there'd never be another like him.

There won't be, unless you try, her practical side admonished. *Remember the feelings, the wild, ecstatic sensations. Soft caresses, bruising lips, eager hands. Nothing, not a single belief in the white world or the red requires you to give them up for the rest of your life. Without them you are an incomplete woman.*

But it hurts so much! How could she ever be herself again?

* * *

12

Springtime had brought out the best in the folks of Litchfield, Nebraska. Men tipped their hats to the ladies, and greeted each other loudly by their first names and a slap on the back. Card games, which had held central interest for these farmers all winter, had diminished to a single table of inveterate players in the back of Cleary's Billiard Palace. There was tilling to do, and plowing for spring wheat. The barely was up knee high and already bindweed threatened to take over the fields. They came in to have McCormick horse-drawn harrow teeth replaced, or mowing machine blades sharpened and to sell eggs and cream. All of this burgeoning business meant satisfying activity at the Farmers' and Homesteaders' Bank of Litchfield.

Which, in turn, attracted the attention of a pair of young men. Their long, lean bodies encased in faded, much washed, Levi Strauss denims, they lounged in front of a saloon. Each wore dark brown, well-worn cartridge belts around their waists, the buttstocks of Colt's Patent Firearms revolvers protruding from loving cared-for holsters. Battered, dusty Stetsons shaded their faces. They wore travel-stained bandanas loosely around their necks. Their long morning of observing traffic in and out of the bank ended when the older of the two dropped the front legs of his captain's chair to the plank porch outside the Sioux Lodge saloon with a bang.

"Satisfied?" Albert Honeycutt inquired of the younger man.

Lane Tulley turned his craggy-jawed face on the

13

pillar of his bull neck and nodded before he spoke. "Looks good to me, Al." He ran thick, blunt fingers through his short, curly black hair. "What say we mosey over and make a withdrawal?"

"I'll bring the horses up from the livery first, Lane," his companion answered. "Best you wait here until I do."

Gray eyes coolly observed the twenty-seven year old Honeycutt. "Whose brother bossed the wildest gang in Dakota Territory? Should be I give the orders."

Al Honeycutt averted his nearly colorless blue eyes to conceal the anger burning in them. "It was only a suggestion, Lane," he said, regretting his deference to the six-foot-two, twenty-two year old he still considered a punk kid.

"All right, then, Al. Why don't you go get the horses, while I keep an eye on the bank?"

"Sure enough," Honeycutt answered with difficulty.

Three minutes later, the pair crossed the dusty main street, stepped up on the boardwalk and tipped their hats to two dowagers passing by. Then they quickly raised their bandanas to cover the lower three-quarters of their faces, drew their sixguns and entered the bank.

"Everyone stand real still and you won't get hurt. This is a holdup," Al Honeycutt announced.

"You there, in the teller's cage. Keep your hands in sight," Lane Tulley commanded. "And you," he addressed to a portly man in a conservative gray suit. "Get a money bag and start fillin' it from that vault."

None of the occupants said a word. Honeycutt stepped to the counter and relieved the two tellers of the contents of their cash drawers, then turned to the patrons. "If you have anything you've just taken out, or where about to put in, please deposit it here," he instructed.

"See here, this is our money, not the bank's," a bespectacled little man in shirtsleeves complained.

"We'll take it anyway. You should feel honored. The Bitter Creek gang is back in action and you're among the first to be robbed," Al added sarcastically.

"Jake Tulley's dead," the banker blurted.

"That might be," Al agreed, then flippantly tacked on, "but his memory lingers on. Cough it up. Everything that jiggles or crinkles."

Lane Tulley walked through the low swinging gate to inspect the vault. "You tried to hold out, old man," he snarled at the banker when he saw a large stack of currency at the rear of the safe.

"Don't take that," the fat man moaned. "It's the payroll for the railroad section hands. A loss like that would ruin the bank. We'd be forced to close."

Steely gray eyes examined him a long moment from above the bandana mask. "That's too bad, fat man. They always say, 'banking is a risky business.' Now hand it over or you die where you stand."

"One shot will bring the marshal and his deputies. The sheriff is in town, too," the banker said defiantly.

Tulley flexed huge, powerful shoulders. "I'll just wring your neck like a chicken," he told the frightened man.

Al Honeycutt stood at the front door. "Get the rest and let's go," he urged.

"In a minute," Lane answered. Then, to the cowed financial officer, "Fill it."

Barely two minutes passed before Lane Tulley stood

at the door. In one hand he held a brass key. Al Honeycutt drew the blinds on both windows and the twin glass panels of the door.

"Now, everyone lie down on the floor. No arguments, do it," the younger outlaw demanded.

They stepped out, Lane locked the door, pocketed the key and they crossed the street briskly to their horses. Reins loosened from the tie-rail, they swung into their saddles in smooth motions. Lane turned the head of his mount to the north and trotted lightly away from the center of town. Al fell in beside him. A block down the street, unobserved by the robbers, a man gave them careful scrutiny.

When the pair rode out of sight of the main street, the lone observer mounted his horse and started out after them. At the same time, glass tinkled musically as someone forced the door of the bank. Five people spilled out onto the street.

"Robbery! The bank's been robbed!" several shouted at once.

The stranger increased his gait and rapidly closed the distance between himself and the holdup men.

An hour before sundown, with an inexperienced posse of farmers and townsmen haring off in the wrong direction, the silent man who had witnessed the departure of the bandits worked his way through a jumble of rocks and tangle of long, slender willow branches. Abruptly he came upon the hidden men and halted, hands raised.

"Hold on now. I ain't come to arrest you, or I'd have had an iron out."

"Then what are you doing here?" Lane Tulley demanded.

"I watched your little performance in Litchfield. You did a smart thing, locking that door and taking the key."

"I don't know what you're talking about," the youthful robber sneered.

"Oh, come now. You did that part well. If I hadn't come along immediately after you, and obliterated your trail, even that posse of yokels would have found you long before now. I'm on your side, really, M'name's Clutter. Loomis Clutter."

"So what is that supposed to mean to us?" Tulley demanded.

"I believe one of you to be Lane Tulley, youngest brother of the late Bitter Creek Jake Tulley?"

"Nope. You got the wrong fellers, Mister Clutter. Best be ridin' on, if ya don't want some new breathin' holes."

"I don't think so. You're the younger of the pair," Clutter said to Tulley, "so I wager you're Lane Tulley. My son, Tom, rode with your brother, Jake. Now, do you think I could step down and pour a cup of that coffee and have a sip? While I do, I can tell you why I've been looking for you, Lane Tulley."

Chapter 2

Insects hummed and buzzed as they darted through the fresh air of a new day. Rebecca Ridgeway had again brought herself to the now-familiar sculpted boulder to sit and contemplate. Despite her near-resolve of the previous afternoon, she found it impossible to open the tightly closed portals of her life and admit others. Herself and Joey, that's all she had left. And even Joey, it seemed, was being inexorably drawn away from her.

He'd become brown as any Oglala, though his snowy hair had a long way to grow before it could be braided. He preferred his Oglala name. *Pinspinzala*, given him by Stands Alone, an uncle by adoption and son of Iron Calf's sister. He had adapted to Sioux clothing in an instant. Declaring joyfully that if he wouldn't get in trouble for it, he'd gladly go naked all the time, instead of being confined in tight shoes, hot, itchy woolen trousers, longjohns and flannel shirts. Unlike Rebecca's own introduction to the band, Joey had eagerly sought to learn the language, and now had an adequate vocabulary for a twelve year old.

Speaking of which — his age, not his language facility — Joey's birthday would be coming soon. In his new culture that meant more than a party and presents. He'd get feasted, true, and receive a horse from Stands Alone, and probably Snow Flower's husband, since he'd taken Badger as his best friend. There would also be the fasting, prayer, and vision-seeking. At least the Army and the reservation agents had forbidden the Sun Dance, the white part of her thought with relief. Joey would not be tempted to torture himself with the thongs and wooden plugs. Rebecca gave a sudden start and tensed at the soft sound of a footstep close behind her.

"You come here too often," Whirlwind declared in a flat tone.

Relieved, yet irritated, Rebecca turned to face him. "You've been watching me?" She immediately felt stupid asking that question, since he obviously had.

"Someone needs to watch over you," Whirlwind answered simply. "I . . . wanted to play my flute outside your lodge," his tone harbored shyness now. "But when I saw the others turned away, without exception, I . . ."

"Whirlwind, I — I'm flattered . . ." *Fool*, her practical side railed.

Tatekohom'ni cloaked his face with misery. "One time, not long ago, we had more together than 'flattery.' "

"Since then, I have had a husband," Rebecca stated coldly.

"And lost him," Whirlwind snapped back. Then his broad, high-cheekboned face crumpled. "That's cruel. I shouldn't have said it. It's only that I . . . I, too, hurt. I lost you when you rode away from the Greasy Grass. I carried a fire close to my heart, in hope it

19

would not be forever."

Rebecca rose and took a hesitant step forward. Then she found herself in Whirlwind's arms. *"Tatekohom'ni*, Whirlwind," she repeated in a tone of misery. "I've tried so hard to — to shut out the hurt, to close myself to . . . to . . ."

"To life?" Whirlwind asked gently.

Suddenly Rebecca began to cry. Something inside let down and the tears flowed without her awareness. She buried her face in Whirlwind's broad shoulder and her thoughts flew over time to the summer on the Greasy Grass. The year her father had died and Custer had been defeated. Whirlwind had fought the soldiers of Custer's Seventh, while she and Lone Wolf had fled possible capture and certain death. Whirlwind had loved her, had shyly confessed to have been in love with her since his boyhood days. She, in turn, gave freely of her body and her emotions to the warrior Whirlwind, who had been but a small boy in her memory. Fate plays strange games, and is always the winner, Rebecca acknowledged. Gradually, her sobs subsided.

"Tell me about it," Whirlwind urged. "Come back to the land of the living."

Haltingly, she began. The words lost their bitterness at this recounting, here in Whirlwind's strong arms. His hands, ever gentle, kept up a constant caress, bringing new quickness to her formerly numbed body. The sun moved two finger-widths while he held her. By then she spoke with ease, relaxed and natural in recounting the events that led to her widowhood. When she described Ezekial Caldwell, Whirlwind interrupted for the first time.

"I will find this one and take his hair."

Surprisingly, Rebecca wanted to laugh. "No need for that, Whirlwind. He is dead. He fell into a large pit of coals and was burned."

"Then your man was avenged and there is no need for you to mourn," Whirlwind said with practicality.

"There is a part of me which is white, Whirlwind, and it grieves."

"There is a part of you which is Dakota, *Sinawka-win*, and needs the love and strength of a man at your side."

And suddenly it was true. Rebecca felt the cold bleakness of her grief melt away and a new, radiant warmth bloom within her body. She began to tremble, filled with an earthy eagerness unlike anything she had experienced in nearly eight months. Whirlwind's fingers conveyed this to him and he drew her closer, pressing her pliant body against the rigid firmness of his hardened flesh. Rebecca gasped.

Restraint, all form of convention fled from her. "Here? Right now?" she asked with roughened breath.

"There's a big pine a short walk from here. There it is soft and fragrant. Let me lead you to it."

It had the aspect of an erotic dream, Rebecca considered as Whirlwind took her hand and started off up a slight slope. Near the crest she saw a lone, tall pine, a symbol of eternity. Her moccasined feet made no sound on the bare earth. She might as well be floating, Rebecca thought. When they reached that spot, Whirlwind spread the robe he carried over his left arm, like all Sioux men, as a sort of badge of his station in the band.

It took no encouraging on Whirlwind's part for

Rebecca to bend and swiftly remove her dress. There was no cause for shyness between them, yet Rebecca felt a strange tingle, like the first time they made love, so long ago. Whirlwind pulled aside his loin cloth, then thought better of it and removed it entirely. Rebecca gasped at the size of his organ. Memory had played her false, she discovered. Naked, they embraced.

"I dreamed often of our being together like this," Whirlwind whispered in her ear.

Rebecca felt the heat of his persistent presence. She laid one hand on his bare chest while the other slid lower. She sighed softly and began to stroke him.

"Aaah," Whirlwind sighed. "You are even more pleasing than before, if that's possible."

"Be tender, because I'm still somewhat afraid," Rebecca pleaded.

"There's nothing to fear now, not here with me, *Sinawkawin*," Whirlwind answered simply.

Folding her legs, she arranged herself on the opened robe.

"Come to me, Whirlwind. Come quickly."

His mighty plunge, that cleaved her to the depths, might have been her deflowering. His heated lance ripped away the last of her sorrow and released her pent-up passions to explode into a wondrous feast of love-making.

Low and leaden, an overcast that drizzled an occasional mist hung over Grand Island, Nebraska. It had no effect on the five men who met in a small, private dining room of the Lawton Hotel. The oldest, Loomis

22

Clutter, address the group.

"With the exception of Al Honeycutt, we all had relatives who rode with Bitter Creek Jake Tulley. And those relations all died at the hands of Rebecca Caldwell or Brett Taylor, the one the Crow call Lone Wolf."

He looked around the faces at the round oak table. Lane Tulley he had come to know over the week since he had caught up to Jake's little brother and Al Honeycutt after the bank robbery. Lane was tough and vicious; at twenty-two, he stood two inches over six feet and weighed two hundred, Loomis estimated. Not an inch of fat, just hard muscle. Matthew Wellington had reached Grand Island the previous evening on the stage. He was twenty-one, and a hair-pin, freely admitting he had been in trouble with the law since the age of ten. Matt wasn't pleasant to look at, his face scarred by smallpox, with a big nose and faded red hair. Of slight build, he was tall and gangly like his late brother.

Of the trio who first responded to his summons, Clutter liked Sheldon Boyle the least. Younger brother of Sonny Boyle, he was a youth of nineteen, with light brown hair, green eyes and a robust physique. Unfortunately, his long, narrow nose and shifty eyes gave him a furtive look that fit well with his reputation as a back-shooter, which had preceded him. Sheldon nodded now, uncomfortable under Clutter's direct gaze.

"In light of past situations, there is little that the five of us might accomplish alone. For that reason, I've spent the last four months contacting those with grievances against the persons I just named." Clutter

23

went on. "There are two others on their way, unavoidably detained by other circumstances. What we need is to learn how many more you might be able to name and-or contact who would join us?"

"Who are the ones coming?" Lane Tulley inquired.

"Patrick O'Toole and Niel Mallory. Paddy O'Toole is a brother of Bobby and Niel is a cousin of Ed Shannon," Loomis answered him.

Tulley frowned. "I'm not too excited about O'Toole. From what my brother used to say, that whole family's shy a few loaves in the bread drawer. That Bobby O'Toole had a thing about carving up little girls."

Expressions of disgust formed on the faces at the table. "We're not interested in anyone's love life," Loomis Clutter snapped. "All that counts is whether that person is willing to help us get revenge on Lone Wolf Baylor and Rebecca Caldwell. They killed my son and three of you lost brothers to them. You wouldn't be here if you didn't believe they deserved punishment. We can overlook some things to get that, I'm sure."

"Count on me," Shell Boyle stated flatly.

"And me," Lane Tulley added.

Clutter produced a bottle from a glassed-in sideboard, set out tumblers. "Then I propose we seal this with a drink."

"What's in it for me?" Al Honeycutt inquired.

"You just acquired five thousand dollars all your own in a bank robbery," Cutter responded. "I consider our force should number some twenty to thirty. To finance such an operation will be costly. No doubt more banks might have to be robbed in order to do so. If you're interested in a share of future earnings, stick around. If not, you're free to leave."

A broad, happy grin spread on Honeycutt's face. "I think I'll stay."

Shiny as a new silver dime, the sun made a tiny bright spot in a cornflower sky. A fresh breeze blew across the rippling grass on the Pine Ridge agency. On a wide, sandy bar in the meandering creek, three Yanktonai Sioux boys, entirely naked, their young bodies glistening with highlights from the sun, applied the finished touches to a cottonwood log raft they had constructed.

"It's almost ready, Young Skunk," one lad declared as he finished weaving a supple willow branch around three logs of thigh thickness.

"We still have the rawhide bindings to put in place," Young Skunk responded, hefting a batch of thin strips lying on the strand.

"Will we go far?" Field Mouse asked solemnly, his eyes big and liquid black.

"Are you afraid, Field Mouse?" Two Hands taunted.

"I am not afraid," Field Mouse pouted. "It's only . . . well, out loincloths and moccasins, ah, what do we do with them?"

Hands on hips, the eldest, Two Hands, frowned and replied, "I told you that before. Can't you hear? We put them in a parfleche bag and carry it on the raft. Long ago, before even the oldest grandfathers left the land beside the big waters, our people used boats made of thin bark to travel everywhere. That way, when they got where they were going, their clothes were dry."

Field Mouse poked out his lower lip. "If we go too far we'll have to walk a long way home."

Two Hands and Young Skunk laughed. "With those rabbit-bone legs of yours, Field Mouse, you could use some walking to build them up," Two Hands declared.

Within twenty minutes, the lads had completed their task. Eager hands joined in to push the vessel off the sand. The crudely crafted conveyance bobbed on the water and struggled to break free.

"Who tries it first to see if it will float?" Field Mouse inquired.

"Why not you?" Young Skunk suggested.

"M-me? I—I don't think I'm heavy enough to make a fair test," Field Mouse deprecated.

"Let's all do it!" Two Hands shouted, tossing the parfleche bag onto the raft and worming his way over the side.

Quickly Young Skunk followed, then, reluctantly, Field Mouse. The current tugged, caught, spun them, then lined the raft out straight in the grip of the stream. The three boys shouted and squealed in delight and self-praise. The banks seemed to blur past. This was better than a horse. Distant lodge tops dwindled from sight. They rounded a bend and familiar camp sounds chopped off as though someone had clapped hands over their ears. On they traveled.

"I wish I could swim this fast," Field Mouse observed.

"You wouldn't want to. You'd scratch your belly on the sand," Two Hands advised.

"How do you know?" Field Mouse demanded.

"I know," the older boy countered flatly.

Dodging low branches and fending off sand bars, the young adventurers covered five miles before they realized it. Even Two Hands began to show an expression of concern. Distracted, he failed to frame a taunting reply to Field Mouse's worried question.

"H-how do we get to shore?"

"We have to ground on a sand bar," Two Hands answered absently. "I—I sure hope there's one around here close."

Another little bend provided for their needs. One corner of the raft ground into the shelf of underwater sand, snagged them momentarily, then the stern of the raft swung out into the center channel.

"Quick, everybody in the water, push hard," Two Hands ordered. "We've got to haul it up ourselves."

Grunting with effort, the three youngsters strained their legs against the creek bed and pushed with all their might. They seemed to gain little. Growing upset, Two Hands looked around.

"Field Mouse, you get out and pull from the front while we push," the oldest of the trio commanded.

"Lift!" he shouted a second later, as the thin eleven year old fought the inertia of sand and logs.

With a lurch, the front of the raft slid forward, to send Field Mouse in a sprawl. The effort had been enough and the swift current of the creek ceased to draw on the vessel. Panting, Two Hands and Young Skunk stumbled to the bar and sank on their haunches.

"We did it," Two Hands gasped out.

"Yes," Field Mouse observed, "and on the wrong side of the creek. We'll have to swim across."

"What's wrong with that?" Young Skunk asked,

27

irritated.

"We'll get our loincloths wet," Field Mouse informed him. "Our moccasins, too. Do you like walking in wet moccasins?"

"Well, look what we got here, boys," a harsh, nasal voice, speaking an alien tongue, interrupted their boyish debate.

Three naked boys spun on the sand and looked among the willows, where three white men sat their horses. Field Mouse put a hand on Young Skunk's shoulder.

"Wasicunpi," he hissed in a whisper.

"Of course," Young Skunk responded. "But they do they want?"

"Nekkid li'l fellers, right outta the water," another of the white men remarked. "You want we should scoop 'em up, Will?"

Will Hardesty studied their find with a jaundiced eye. All about eleven or twelve, two of them at least muscular enough to do. He shrugged.

"Might as well, 'Miah. They're all the catch we're likely to come upon today."

Nehemiah Logan and Victor Parks dismounted and walked toward the boys. As one, the copper-skinned trio began to scuttle across the sand toward the water. Logan drew his sixgun.

"Unh-unh. No runnin' away now," he warned.

Unaware that the whites dare not fire their weapons, the boys froze. Victor and Nehemiah quickly bound their hands behind them with rawhide. Then the elder, Victor, studied their nakedness.

"You got any clothes?" he asked, making the sign for loincloth.

28

"O-o-on the raft," Field Mouse stammered in Lakota.

"What?" Victor questioned.

Two Hands pointed with his chin. "On the raft. In the parfleche," he stated clearly in his own language.

"I think he means that parfleche on the raft," Will Hardesty suggested.

Nehemiah found the boys' loincloths and moccasins. To his disgust, he got the duty of putting the items on each boy.

"After all, you're the one that's had kids before," Will Hardesty informed him. "You oughtta know how to dress 'em."

That accomplished, they sat the boys together on a bareback horse, tied their feet together under its belly, and started off. "Not too bad, considerin'," Victor observed.

"How you mean?" Nehemiah growled.

"We've got us a good business goin', 'Miah," Victor explained. "We got to keep our customers satisfied. We have three fresh boys to sell, which is good. Onlyest bad thing is we didn't rustle up a few little girls this trip. Lotta'll sure be disappointed."

Chapter 3

Dust, borne on a following wind, enveloped the stage coach when it halted abruptly on the Western Nebraska plain. Passengers coughed and complained and failed at first to hear the cause of the sudden stop.

"Whatever is the matter with you, driver?" a buxom matron demanded in an annoyed tone.

"You're being robbed, lady, if you really want to know," a voice came from outside the coach.

Curtain-like, the dust raised and departed on the breeze. Mrs. Purvis Ackerly pulled aside the leather roll shade and looked out to see some seven masked men at her side of the stage. She let out a frightened squawk and promptly fainted. Her plump bulk fell across the lap of Myron Claggett, a sales representative of the Arbuckle Coffee Company.

"Oh, dear, what do I do now?" he asked in concern.

"Wave your hat at her face," a painted-face woman, with the lines of hard living etched vertically into her cheeks, offered. "Maybe that will revive her. Too bad you ain't a whiskey drummer. A little snort would do the trick right proper."

"Heaven forbid," Mrs. Ackerly declared in a shuddering sigh. "Spiritous liquors shall ne'er touch these lips." Her obligatory denunciation of Demon Rum duly delivered, she again lapsed into her comatose state.

"So that's what's wrong with her?" the coffee salesman announced. "Teetotalers ain't got any sand. With a good snort of Hill and Hill, I'd take on these ruffians single-handed."

"Wouldn't do you half as much good as this Colt," a youngish man across the interior told Claggett as he patted his coat, which concealed a cartridge belt, holster and sixgun.

"You have a firearm? Why aren't you using it, then?" an indignant Claggett charged.

"Because I've got no great hanker to be turned into a sieve. By my reckoning, there must be near a dozen of them out there."

A sort of wet, blubbery sigh came from Mrs. Ackerly. The next instant, the door opened and a masked man confronted the passengers. He gestured with the blue steel barrel of his Remington .44 revolver.

"Everybody out. Move it out!" he barked.

Within five minutes, the coffee salesman and other passengers had been relieved of their money and valuables, and left standing in the dust beside the high wheels of the Concord coach. Two strongboxes had been given up, somewhat reluctantly, by the driver and guard. They, too, stood on the ground. The leader of the robbers gave a satisfied nod. He and his men mounted up, the heavy boxes lashed to the pack

31

frame on a stout mule. Before they departed, the stocky man with the pale, yellow-green eyes edged his mount up close to the coach and used his Colt's .45 to shoot the wheeler horse in its traces.

"That oughtta slow you down a little in reporting this, folks," he informed the shocked victims. "Good day, now."

Clive Hennesy closed his bank in Mullen, Nebraska promptly at four o'clock each afternoon. The sudden arrival of what appeared to be five more customers at one minute before the hour disturbed him considerably. By rights, he figured, he should inform them that the bank was closing and to come back the next day. He decided to do just that, when the quintet drew bandana masks over their faces and produced weapons.

"Stand fast and no one will get hurt!" a stocky man with oddly yellow-green eyes demanded. "This is a holdup."

Hennesy's bank had two guards, one in the open, to supervise the lobby, the other hidden behind a partition, reinformed with sandbags. They had their instructions regarding robberies and the president of the First Prairie Bank felt confident they would follow them to the letter.

Vance Neighbors did, to Clive Hennesy's relief. The guard stepped back against a wall, to appear more unobtrusive, and raised his hands. Behind his section of wall, above the teller's cages, Ned Pickering fingered the receiver of his Winchester and used the peep-hole to choose his first target.

Two of the holdup men stood at the door, sixguns ready. The other three went about the business of emptying the teller's trays and looting the vault. Fortunately only two customers had been caught inside when the robbery started. Secure and confident in his mini-fortress, Ned decided to take out the visible outlaws, at the door, then wait for the others to show themselves. Carefully he eased his rifle into position.

Blam! The flat discharge of the Winchester battered the ears of everyone in the building. The heavy slug smacked into the hollow of Thad Greene's throat, spraying blood in a wide fan around the bank. He slammed back against the door, breaking a glass panel, and his body drooped awkwardly over the sharp shards in the casement. Before any of the outlaws could react, Ned levered in a fresh cartridge and fired again.

Answering rounds slammed into the lowered ceiling behind the tellers' cages, ripping wooden splinters from the floor around Ned's chair. His own shot missed and he cycled the Winchester, mindful of the bullets that cracked past so close to him. Vance Neighbors saw his chance and took it. He drew, crouched and fired his Smith American.

Hot lead split a chunk from the frontpiece of the teller's counter close to Loomis Clutter's face. A sliver struck him and produced a small blood spot. Loomis turned a quarter way toward the distant wall and fired his Remington. He dead-centered the bank guard, who propelled himself backward, to slam against the wainscoting and slide to a sitting position, leaving a wide, wet, red smear. Immediately, Loomis began to issue orders.

"Take what you've got and let's get out of here. Lane, cover us 'till we clear the door."

Lane Tulley nodded and snapped off a shot to the left of where he saw a muzzle flash in the facing above the tellers' cages. From behind it he heard a grunt and the sound of something heavy falling to the floor. One-by-one the outlaws withdrew from the bank. Lane Tulley came last, firing his final two rounds wildly toward the cluster of frightened employees.

Outside, he paused to eject spent cartridges and fill his cylinder with new. Patrick O'Toole held his horse by the reins and Lane Tulley ran that way as shots barked from down the street. He swung into the saddle and the gang raced in the opposite direction. Lane and Paddy turned at their waists and threw quick shots at the lawmen running behind them. With a loud rumble over a wooden bridge, they stormed out of town and away from danger. Lane allowed himself a sigh of weariness. They'd hit the stage coach and a bank.

Two holdups in the same day might be a bit more than wise. Tulley considered. They'd lost a man, but the bank had two killed. How much they made, he wasn't sure. Every bit would help, though. When they reached Pierre, in Dakota Territory, they would be joined by more relatives of former gang members and the hunt would begin in earnest.

"When did you first hear of this?" Rebecca Caldwell Ridgeway asked Whirlwind.

"Only this morning. Indian Police come from Ma-

jor Storey. They had a message for our chiefs." Whirlwind paused and scowled heavily. "Such things make
me want to kill all white men."

Rebecca placed a hand on his. "I can understand
your feelings, Whirlwind. This is an awful thing.
Children being taken from the reservations. Why?
Where are they taken? What for?"

Whirlwind quirked his lips into a sad smile. "You
ask many questions. If only you had the answers."

"Tell me more," Rebecca urged.

"Our children are being stolen by someone. Shod
hoofs say white men. Boys and girls alike are taken.
They simply disappear and are never seen or heard of
again. So far it has been at least thirty."

"White couples wouldn't want to raise Indian children," Rebecca reasoned aloud. "There's too much
prejudice. They wouldn't pay for getting them, so no
profit. What reason then?"

"I wish I knew," Whirlwind responded gloomily.

"I want to go see Major Storey," the white squaw
decided suddenly. "Maybe he can tell us more."

Half an hour's ride brought the pair to the agency
headquarters. Mrs. Amellia Storey made then welcome in the parlor and summoned her husband,
Harvey. "He's been working in the garden," she explained. "I've had the devil's own time getting him to
turn it over for me. I'll be right back."

Amellia Storey had provided coffee and they sipped
in silence for a few minutes. At last, Harvey Storey, a
retired Army major, entered. He nodded greeting to
Rebecca and spoke first to Whirlwind in the Lakota
tongue.

"We've come about the missing children," Whirlwind answered him.

"I see. What is it I can do?" Storey asked.

Rebecca, much to the agent's surprise, took up the story. "We'd like to know everything you have found out so far."

Storey recalled that there was a half-breed woman living among the Red Top Lodge band, the widow of a prominent Territorial rancher named Ridgeway. "You must be Mrs. Ridgeway?"

"Yes I am, but call me Rebecca, Major Storey. Only today I became aware of this situation and would like to know more."

"To what end?"

"Finding the persons responsible, punishing them and getting the children back if possible," Rebecca stated positively.

"That's quite an undertaking," Major Storey said dryly.

"Perhaps you are not aware, Major Storey, that I have considerable background at hunting down people."

"Well, now, Mrs. Ridgeway, ah . . ."

"I started with the Bitter Creek Jake Tulley gang, if you recall them?" Rebecca interruped demurely. "There used to be forty of them. Now, only Roger Styles is left. Two of the gang were my uncles. I killed them both. That was the white part of me, seeking retribution for what was done to my mother and myself. Now, my Sioux part wants to do something to help my people."

Embarrassment colored Storey's face. "I, ah, I didn't quite realize, Mrs., ah, Miss Rebecca. What can I do to help?"

"Thank you, Harvey. I need to know from where, the number and when these children disappeared. Also, I would like to know what is being done by whom to rescue them. That will give me a place to start."

Major Storey related all of the information he had regarding the matter. When he finished, Rebecca continued to look thoughtfully at his craggy features as though expecting more. He sighed heavily.

"You can see there's little or nothing to go on. How do you propose going about it?"

"Did you note, Harvey," Rebecca replied, "that all of the children have so far been taken from agencies close to the Black Hills? It could be that's where the missing youngsters are going, or because of the proximity of the Nebraska line. I think a visit to the scene is in order. That way I can talk with the parents, with whomever discovered the exact location from which they were taken. All of that information has to add up to something."

"Yes, yes, you're right, Miss Rebecca," Storey allowed. "I have to admit that the largest problem so far is that there simply isn't anyone in an official capacity, with the time or authority to look into the matter, or who is inclined toward investigating the loss of a group of Indian children. *I* would, if I could. And I wish you well. Now, if you haven't anything else pressing, my wife would like you two to stay to dinner. It's close to noon and I know you must be hungry."

"Thank you, Harvey. We'll do that. Then, tomorrow at the latest, I want to start for the Pine Ridge reservation," Rebecca agreed.

* * *
37

Shakes-the-Ground looked with contempt at the woman in the beaded white elkhide dress and the warrior beside her. What sort of man would let a woman do his talking? What sort of woman would want to humiliate a man in such a way. Rebecca Caldwell Ridgeway, the subject of his scorn, soon realized that she would get nothing useful from this over-proud civil chief. She accepted defeat gracefully, muttered her thanks and departed. At least, among the women, she might get cooperation.

"No woman talks with Shakes-the-Ground," a fat older lady of the Sansarc told Rebecca later. "Not even his wives," she added with a chuckle. "He believes no woman is good enough to talk to any man. So they talk to each other within his hearing to let their wishes and needs be known. He will not help you, nor will any of the men. They hate it here at the agency and take it out on us. Go see Willow, in the Hunkpapa hoop. She lost a boy only two moons ago. Listen to her. Your young man," she said with a twinkle in her eye, pointing with her chin, "wears the mark of the Badger Society. There is a lodge of them among us, also. He can learn things there."

"Thank you, Bright Comb," Rebecca returned sincerely. "May I use your name in speaking with these other persons?"

"Wagh! Use it, for what good that might be. In the days before this place, we would have made these child stealers pay. Oh! I remember how that was." Her wrinkled face grew wet with tears as Bright Comb bid Rebecca success and returned to her tipi.

Later that night, in a borrowed lodge, Rebecca lay in Whirlwind's arms, body vibrantly alive from their recent lovemaking, mind working over the information she had gleaned. It came to precious little. Hopefully, she laid a finger on Whirlwind's chest.

"What did you hear from your *Ihoka* brothers?" she inquired.

"Only what we expected. The child stealers are white men. They cover their tracks well and always pick children who are alone and far from the villages. From here their trail leads always to the river. They must use a boat in order to confuse anyone following."

"That indicates some sort of organization and planning. Only why? What do they get out of stealing Sioux children?"

"Some of the old people claim that this is a punishment for the people for having abandoned the old ways and moved to the reservations," Whirlwind added after a moment's thought.

"Do you believe that?" Rebecca probed, uncertain of her own mixed feelings, which might invalidate her decision.

"Of course not. The Badger Society war chief here believes there is a far worse reason behind it."

"What is that?" Rebecca queried.

"There have always been slaves among the people. Red Leaf suspects that these missing ones are being taken for that purpose."

"Among whites?" Incredulous, Rebecca could not accept this concept. "There was a big war fought among the whites that ended slavery. Their own people will not allow anyone to openly keep slaves."

"The white man's laws are spread thinly out here,"

39

Whirlwind suggested.

"We have to visit three more agencies. After we talk with them, we'll consider that possibility. But slavery, Whirlwind? This could be far more dangerous than we expected," Rebecca stated in a worried tone.

Chapter 4

Sickly sweet, the acrid smoke of burning flesh rose from the ex-soldier's belly. The pale, white flesh blackened where it touched a glowing, walnut-sized coal. Blistered and reddened, encrusted with drying blood, half a dozen similar spots showed on his savaged body. Neck corded, mouth wide in torment, he screamed in agony as yet another coal dropped upon his abdomen. Sweat-soaked, his graying brown hair hung lank around his battered head.

"We know you was friendly with him. Might as well cough it up now. Where'd Lone Wolf Baylor go?" Ike MacKinnon purred softly.

Starlight twinkled weakly in a Dakota sky that wore a fine veil of high, light cloud. Loomis Clutter and Lane Tulley sat near by. They had taken the gang to Pierre and waited two days until, Isaac MacKinnon, Raymond Dawson, and Peter Dillon had joined them. Others came soon after. Now they numbered twenty. Lane Tulley had encountered a retiring Army sergeant who had spoken of knowing Lone Wolf.

Enticed into a drinking bout, the ex-soldier and a civilian friend, also acquainted with Lone Wolf, were jollied into a state of blind, staggering drunkenness. Lane Tulley and three of the gang spirited them off from the streets of Pierre. They had come to this location, a folded arroyo at the base of a tall, stately bluff. Then the torture had begun. The civilian had died a quarter hour ago, remaining steadfast in his denial of any information on Baylor or Rebecca Caldwell. Now Ike MacKinnon and Paddy O'Toole practiced the crudest of torments upon the remaining victim.

"He's lost a lot of blood," Lane Tulley remarked. "Don't want to lose him like we did the other. 'Least not before we find out what we want."

"Burning don't bleed 'em none," Paddy O'Toole responded, lifting a savage face from the fireside. "What I oughtta do is pinch off his toes, one at a time."

A gagging sound came from their prisoner. Paddy glanced back at him and dropped a third coal, onto his chest this time. The ex-sergeant howled and arched his back, rawhide cutting into his wrists and ankles.

"Where is he, damn you?" Lane Tulley demanded.

"Not . . . not around here," the weakening man gasped.

"Where?" MacKinnon bellowed, spittle from his lips spraying the man.

"Don' know. N-not for s-s-sure," came a weak reply.

"Tell us, or the next coal goes on your pecker," Paddy O'Toole put in with a giggle.

"C-can't say. I . . . I . . . aaaaaayieeeeeaaaahh! No-no-nomore! D-don't do any more to me."

"Help us find Lone Wolf Baylor and we'll stop all

this," Lane Tulley urged in a coaxing tone.

"He . . . he's gone completely Injun. He's taken to something religious of the Crows," came a babbled reply. "Last I heard, he was in some secret canyon on the east slopes of the Black Hills. Doin' a lot of praying and singing, that sort of thing."

"Where is the Hills?" Tulley demanded.

"I dunno. Believe me, I don't," the torture victim begged.

"Black Hills?" Clutter inquired in a disinterested tone.

"Yeah."

"Eastern slopes?" Clutter again.

"S-sure. Gotta pray to the sun or something like that," the suffering man responded.

"No foolin' on this?" Paddy O'Toole asked, another coal poised in tongs above the writhing man's chest. "I'll drop this one on your face."

"I swear to God! That's all I know. B-Black Hills. He's there, somewhere."

"Thank you, my man," Loomis Clutter said politely, a moment before he lined up his sixgun and shot the ex-sergeant between the eyes.

Rebecca Caldwell's inquiry into the missing Sioux children had been interrupted by an urgent message from an old and dear friend. Buell Holbert, and his wife Gloria, had aided Rebecca early in her quest to bring retribution to Jake Tulley and his gang. They had sheltered her and provided funds when needed. When the message reached her from Gloria that Buell was seriously ill and not expected to live, she went

43

immediately to the Rosebud reservation and made arrangements to travel to their home in northwestern Nebraska.

"But, Mom," Joey protested, when he learned her plans. "Why can't I come with you?"

"Buell Holbert isn't expected to survive his sickness, Joey. He . . . well, you've seen enough to death and sorrow for a while. God knows we both have. I feel it would be better if you remained here."

Face twisted in momentary hurt, Joey spun away from her and started for the entrance to their lodge. He collided with Whirlwind.

"Ho! Where are you headed, *Pinspinzala?*"

"Why do *you* care?" Joey snapped, releasing his frustration on the handsome young Oglala, who now openly vied with the lad for Rebecca's affection.

"Because I came to take you hunting with me," Whirlwind answered simply. "Why do I find you with your head filled with thunderclouds?"

When the warrior's words registered, Joey brightened considerably. "Hunting? Is *Hoka* coming along?"

"Yes, if you want. You'll be staying with Brave Elk and Snow Flower while your mother is gone. So, that makes *Hoka* your brother of sorts for a while, and I don't doubt he'll want to go with us."

"I'll go tell him," Little Prairie Dog Ridgeway piped in excitement as he exited through the low doorway of the tipi.

Rebecca appeared bemused. "He seems to have forgotten he was angry at me for leaving him behind," she observed.

Whirlwind smiled. "Small boys love their mothers deeply, but hunting is another matter."

"You're so kind to us," Rebecca declared, laying a hand on Whirlwind's arm. "I'm afraid I haven't enough experience at mothering."

"You'll learn. And my kindness is because I want you for my wife."

Of a sudden, Rebecca's mood changed, her expression darkening. "Don't talk of that now, please, Whirlwind. It's . . . too soon. I . . ."

"It has been nearly a year," he offered, a bit stiffly.

"I know. Only . . . bear with me in this. I have to be honest . . . I don't know if I can ever seriously consider marriage again."

Her words brought a frown to Whirlwind's high, smooth forehead. "I'll wait for your answer. I haven't any choice. Only, don't think that way. At least not now. Hold open your heart."

Touched by his simple protest of undying love, Rebecca relented a little. She rose on tiptoe and kissed Whirlwind lightly on one cheek. "I will," she said sincerely. Then turned away to gather her white world clothing. "Right now I must hurry and pack. Watch after Joey for me."

"I will. He'll be kept so busy he won't have time to realize you're gone."

For three days after Rebecca left for the Holbert home, Joey indeed showed little sign of missing his step-mother. He launched himself into the life of the camp, becoming *Pinspinzala* more thoroughly than ever before. He and Badger, along with *Mahtolasan* and *Pangeca*, another of Joey's friends, ranged the hills of the reservation. They went fishing and swimming, and often hunted with Whirlwind and his friend, *Nugepitanka*, Big Ears. The warriors were young enough to remember what it meant to be a small boy and entered into the lads' high-spirited activities without condescension. When a week had gone by, *Pinspinzala* and his friends roamed more often on their own.

On one such occasion they went to a quiet bend of the creek to catch fresh water mussels and crayfish for a special soup *Wahca Wahin* had promised her son *Hoka* and Joey. They all squatted in the shallow water when four white men quietly approached. Badger sensed their presence first and tensed, making the sign for quiet to the others.

Their caution came too late. With fast steps, Will Hardesty and his ruffians grabbed the wet, wriggling boys and twisted their hands behind them. Hard, callused fingers stoppered their mouths until bandanas replaced them. Kicking wildly, Joey, Badger, *Pangeca* and Tommy were taken to horses some distance along the creek bank.

"We got us a couple of renegades here," Will observed, nodding toward Joey and Tommy.

"That or some Swede soljer's been humpin' the squaws," one of his men observed.

"What do you want with us?' Joey demanded, wise enough to speak the Oglala tongue.

"Speak English, ya little bastard," Will snarled.

"I don't know what you're saying," Joey responded again in Lakota.

Mahtolasan caught on and gave a little nod to his friend. If these men didn't know they were understood, maybe it would help them. That, at least, he figured Joey to be thinking.

"Load 'em up," Will commanded. "Two to a horse.

46

Then we'll go pick up the others. Whooeee, we got us a good load this time. This makes seven from the Rosebud alone. All prime, too."

"Good thing we got those gals over 't other side of the camp," Ed Miller observed. "Lotta's gonna like them plenty."

"She's getting frantic," Will replied. "Goes through those Sioux gals mighty fast in them bawdy houses of hers. Funny, she says, the way they up and die on her."

"Don't reckon it's funny to them," Vic Parks snickered.

Joey and *Mahtolasan* exchanged glances. They knew well what bawdy houses were.

But he didn't know as yet what they did with the boys they captured. Abruptly, their course descended into a ragged-walled arroyo, where two more white men waited with a rough dozen Sioux boys and girls. The one who must be the leader hailed the others.

"We got us some more boy-brats to sell them miners, Norm," Will Hardesty called.

Sell to miners? Joey questioned silently.

"Nice haul, Boss," Norm Watson, the man beside a low fire stated.

"Put out that fire and we'll head for the Hills," Will ordered. "In two days we'll be spendin' money like drunken sailors."

It all seemed like a dream. Now that his fasting and prayer had ended, Lone Wolf saw clearly the visions his state had brought him. It was his past life, that of a white man, which faded to unreality. He worked slowly about his spartan camp. First he destroyed the sacred sweat lodge, then packed his scant belongings. When the fire lowered so that he could cook, he would eat his first meal in five days. Already the carcass of the large red squirrel had been fastened to a stick and rested against a smooth rock beside the flickering blaze.

Gazing into the flames, Lone Wolf spoke aloud as he attempted to recall the long ago days when he was known as Brett Baylor . . .

. . . Tall, blond and handsome, newly married and just turned twenty-three, Brett Baylor had come to the Nebraska plains to build a home and a new way of life. His homestead had fared well and his service with the Union Army during the War had insured him benefits in claiming new ground in the Dakotas when they opened up. He rented his place to a sharecropper and moved his wife, swelling with a new life within her, to Dakota.

There they made a house of log and sod blocks. Brett built a corral, and later a barn. Then the Crows came raiding. Their target had been the Sioux, but they detoured long enough to attack an offending white man's home. Brett had been hunting, he recalled with difficulty. From a great distance he saw the column of smoke. Heart racing, he went full speed to his homestead.

He arrived in time to see the Crow warriors brutally murder his wife and the unborn babe. By then the house had also been set ablaze. Brett, that other Brett of so long ago, had attacked the raiding party with blind ferocity. Unmindful of the numbers, he threw himself at them, killing five before his rifle stripped a casing in the chamber. Even then he used it as a club, braining two more warriors before they subdued him. Admiration for his courage kept Brett alive. The Crow took him with them.

In their home village, he was subjected to humiliation and torment, until he challenged the biggest warrior and defeated him. He received a new name then, Lone Wolf, and began to learn the language. For ten years he rode with the Crow, fought their battles with them and took a woman. He had two children, a boy who would be in his teens, and girl, eleven. Yet, when the opportunity came in, in the Oglala camp of Iron Calf, he abandoned it all and escaped with Rebecca Caldwell.

Theirs had been a platonic relationship. Rebecca, filled with rage and grief, had no thoughts for a man. Lone Wolf had earlier begun his long path to the Power Road of Crow mysticism, which required him to be celibate. Also, when they met, he was nearly old enough to be her father. At thirty-three, he had fifteen years on her. Since that time, their friendship had become comfortable and familiar, without overtones of lust or desire. Each pursued what they wanted. Rebecca's love affair with Grover Ridgeway had been an unexpected event. Lone Wolf had taken the opportunity that her impending marriage had offered to at last undertake the spiritual awakening necessary to his goal.

Having achieved that now, these more recent events remained clearer. Would his next elevation, to the threshold of the Power Road, wipe out even more of

49

his past? Would he eventually cease to live at all on this plane of existence, as the medicine men said?

And if so, what would his new way of life be like? Slowly the mists of the past closed in on his reflections . . .

. . . Time and enough, Lone Wolf decided, to fix his meal, fill his belly and be on his way. First he would have to report to old Burning Star, his Crow medicine man spirit guide. Then he would look into the future.

Chapter 5

Three families of wrens chirped happily in the apartment birdhouse Buell Holbert had built for them and Gloria, his wife of thirty years, lovingly tended. A robin warbled and long tree shadows fell over the neat, square, white house. At the kitchen table, Rebecca Caldwell Ridgeway sat with Gloria Holbert, drinking coffee from delicate, thin china cups.

"You mean to say that you've finally given up your quest for revenge?" Gloria inquired in a sweet, elderly voice.

The subject of their conversation, logically enough, was Rebecca's years-long battle with the Jake Tulley gang. It discomfited Rebecca some, yet she willingly discussed it since she knew Gloria would otherwise dwell on her dying husband. That they could both do without. On Rebecca's arrival, they had had a sisterly cry over it, visited his sickroom, and talked of the onset of his terminal condition.

During the week they had spoken of many things and only occasionally diverted to Buell Holbert and his illness. With most topics well covered, the cause that had first brought these people together came up.

"Yes. Actually, I had determined to abandon the chase considerably earlier. Back when I felt certain that only Roger Styles remained, and he far off in Mexico. Before then I had pursued elements of the gang as far as California."

With careful attention to detail, Rebecca outlined the most recent years of her revenge. She spoke of her time in Oregon with the Nez Perce, and of the journey southward to Yuma, in Arizona Territory. Likewise of her escapade in San Diego, where she almost finished off Roger Styles.

"You would absolutely adore Alonzo Horton. He is old money and old style. He has a beautiful mansion on a promontory overlooking the new town of San Diego," Rebecca revealed to her hostess. "Horton is a business man and a land speculator. Also the number one promoter of San Diego. He has this courtly way of speaking and charms all the ladies." Rebecca's details went on.

She described the battle in Northern California against the hired guns of the railroad magnates, her Uncle Ezekial included. When she spoke of leaving him stranded in Donner Pass, the ache within began to expand for the first time in nearly a month. She recounted how she had come to meet, then fall in love with Grover Ridgeway, all the while her pain welled up.

"He was a dear, devoted man, with two sons," Rebecca confided to her elderly friend. "Young, virile, a remarkable lover and a shrewd rancher. He loved me long before I realized that I had begun to fall in love with him. Grover asked me to marry him and I couldn't find the words to tell him no. In fact, I couldn't bear the thought of rejecting his proposal."

Gloria Holbert patted her hand. "Now, that's the way love's supposed to be, Becky. Ah, I remember how overpoweringly in love I was with Buell. Still am, for that matter. Every day seemed more wonderful than the one before."

"That's how it was with us," Rebecca agreed. "Nothing, I felt, could ever come between us. I found a happiness I thought I'd never have. And then . . ."

"What, dear?"

Anguish lay under the creamy-bronze skin of Rebecca's face. Her friend could read it in her eyes. "Then Uncle Ezekial came back. He had survived the winter by . . . eating . . . like the Donners did," loathing warred with grief on Rebecca's face and in her words. "He came eastward, hunting me. Everywhere he went, he killed people. Murdering someone meant nothing to him. He found out where I had moved and came out to the ranch after me. Ezekial fought with Grover and killed him. Then he killed Grover's older son, Peter. I—I went berserk. We struggled and somehow went out a window onto the lawn. Ezekial came after me with a knife after I cut him and he lost his gun. Then . . . then he grabbed Joey as a hostage. By that time Ezekial and Joey stood on the edge of a barbecue pit.

"Oh, a huge thing in which a couple of steers had been roasted for a party," Rebecca recounted, arms moving wide in illustration. "Joey bit him and leaped away. Ezekial fell backward into the pit. He burned to death before anyone could move to save him."

"Well and good, if you ask me," Gloria Holbert responded with surprising iciness. "I never could abide Ezekial Caldwell or that ne'er do well brother of his, Virgil. I only hope that his tumble into those coals was a foretaste of what he'll have to endure for eternity." She nodded sharply in affirmation. "More coffee, Becky? I do have to get busy on those pies I'm to make today."

"No more for me, thanks," Rebecca begged off.

"Then it's off to the storm cellar for canned cherries," Gloria suggested.

"Before you do, Gloria," the doctor announced as he entered through the hall doorway, "I think you ladies should come with me. Buell's condition has taken a turn for the worse. I'm sorry."

Since leaving the area of the reservations, the gags had been removed from each of the children. They could shout all they wanted, they had been told, all it would get them was a riding crop across the shoulders. One of the men who had captured them could speak Lakota, not well but enough to convey orders. Between that and the undisclosed knowledge of English Joey and Tommy possessed, the captives kept well informed. When they reached the Black Hills, the adopted white boys began to worry.

"We'll never get back from here without help," Joey confided to his companions.

"Will we be together?" Badger inquired.

"Who knows?" Tommy answered uneasily.

At the first stop, they learned their fate when two boys were sold to a hard-faced miner, who paid in gold and shoved his purchases off to a low, crudely built hovel beside a mine entrance. Several of the girls began to cry as the cavalcade rode off under the trees.

"Where was that one-eyed miner, he an' his partner wanted three?" Will Hardesty inquired of his men.

"Not far now," came the answer from Ed Miller. "Over near Alder Gulch. Red Tyback an' Mule-Ear Johnson."

"That's them. We'll stop by and then take the girls to Lotta," Hardesty decided. "Then deal with the rest."

"How about Colter? He wanted two, an' it's right by Tyback's claim," Victor Parks suggested.

"Fine. That stocky tow-head and his two pals can go to Tyback an' the other breed to Colter," Hardesty decided.

Nehemiah Logan gave a low chuckle. "Maybe them breeds'll last a bit longer."

Joey puzzled over that remark while the group trotted through the cool shade beneath tall pines, ash and aspen. They came upon the Colter claim shortly after noon. A small man, with gimlet eyes and a hard mouth, examined the offering with considerable doubt.

"This one's got a cast in his eye," he complained about a Sioux boy from another reservation.

"Don't keep him from digging," Will Hardesty said dryly.

"Might be he's sickly," Colter came back.

"Nope. Sound as a dollar. An' what about this one? He's a little skinny, but strong," Hardesty indicated Tommy while he spoke. "Got a bit of white blood in him, might even be able to learn human speech."

"That'd be a blessin'," Colter conceded. "I'll take 'em."

"Done and good. Hunnerd dollars each, in gold."

55

At a nod from Hardesty, the Sioux boy and Tommy were cut out of the rest. *"Mahtolasan!"* Joey called to him, shocked by the rude separation.

"Remember where I am," Tommy answered in Lakota. "Somehow we'll escape."

Joey had no difficulty keeping track of their journey from Colter's to where another bargain was struck. This time, a man with a patch over one eye, gnarled hands, graying red hair and a long, tobacco juice-streaked, carroty beard picked Badger, *Pangeca,* and Joey. As the remaining captives rode away, despair rose and threatened to overwhelm Joey. He brushed angrily at a tear that escaped one eye and faced his "owner" defiantly.

"You unnerstan' what I'm sayin', boy?" Red Tyback growled.

His pale blue eye took in the clean, stocky lines of Joey's body with appreciation. This one could do some work, all right. Joey stared at him blankly. Too swift to be avoided, a hand lashed out and smacked against Joey's cheek.

"Answer me, boy. Yer eyes are bluer than mine an' hair white as snow. The woman who popped you out weren't no squaw. Could be she was a captive, eh? An' you brought up an Injun kid? Any way you slice it, it's still fatback. So you know what I'm sayin', don't you?"

Again Joey refused any answer. Tyback backhanded him again. His partner, Mule-Ear Johnson appeared at the mine entrance.

"Take it easy, Red. Break his jaw, he won't be any good to us."

"Just tryin' to get his attention, Porter," Red responded. "I feel it in my bones, he knows everything we're sayin'."

"Looks like you made a good buy," Johnson observed, in an attempt to get his partner's attention off the white-haired boy. "These other two got a lot of strength, like him."

Tyback beamed. "Yep. Wickered Hardesty good this time. Now, if we can get 'em to work . . ."

"Let me try," Mule-Ear suggested. "Boy, you've got too much intelligence sparklin' in them blue eyes. You do know every word we say, right? Reckon I know why you played dumb. Didn't want them that caught you up to know you understood what they said, that it?"

"How'd you kn—" Joey blurted out before he could stop himself.

"There you are!" Mule-Ear rejoiced. "Knowed it all along. Can't blame you for that at all. But things is changed now. You'll get along a lot better if you talk to us, help your friends there to know what we want."

"What *do* you want?" Joey asked in a surly tone.

"Why, for you three to work our mine. There's a lot of blue granite in that hill, and only a thin little vein of ore. It's been gettin' narrower and narrower, to the point we two can't fit in there any more. Little fellers like you wouldn't have any trouble a-tall. Yer to open it up some while bringing out the gold." Mule-Ear studied Joey's face a moment. "How long you been with the Sioux?"

"About a year," Joey admitted.

"What's yer name?" Johnson asked.

"Pinspinzala," came the simple answer.

Unable to abide this gush of kindness longer, Tyback reached out and shook Joey by one shoulder. "Yer white name, damnit!"

"Go easy, Red," Mule-Ear spoke softly. "Go on, son."

"J-Joey. Ridgeway."

Johnson's eyebrow raised over his glittering left orb. "Any relation to Grover Ridgeway, down Murdo country?"

"He—he was my paw," Joey answered through a tight throat.

"I heard he'd been done in somehow. We can go into how you got to be with the Sioux later. For now, all I want is for you to help make clear to your friends what it is we want."

Hands on hips, Joey asked defiantly, "What if I don't?"

Mule-Ear produced a nasty chuckle. "Then I'll turn you over to Red here and let him use that bullwhip on you."

Joey swallowed with some difficulty and felt a powerful urge to empty his bladder. He looked from one miner to the other, swallowed again. "What do we have to do?"

"For one thing, you'll get to learn how to shoot powder."

"I know how to use a gun," Joey responded.

"I mean blastin'. Dynamite, that sort of thing."

Joey's eyes grew wide and round. "I . . . will?"

"Yep. My word on it. Now, how about some food? While I work on 'em, how about you tell these boys what's in store," Johnson concluded, starting for a rock-ringed cookfire near the small dwelling.

Filled with excitement over the prospect of learning

to use explosives, Joey explained their situation to Badger and *Pangeca*. Soon the odor of frying bacon and potatoes filled the air. Joey's stomach growled and his companions caught some of his excitement.

Only a single day of back-breaking labor in the mine convinced Joey that their future didn't hold quite so bright a picture as Mule-Ear's words described. Foul air and rock dust made them pant. Their bodies, naked except for loincloth and moccasins, grew slicked with sweat and coated with yellow-gray. Blisters developed on their fingers and palms, broke and new ones rose up. They bled from multiple cuts and abrasions. So far, Joey had not even seen a stick of dynamite. He wanted to throw himself on the ground and bawl like a baby.

Pride and the necessity to help his friends kept him from it. After ten grueling hours, Johnson summoned them from the black hole in the ground. "Crick's over there. Go wash up and eat yer supper," he commanded tersely.

Gratefully, the three boys staggered to the stream and immersed themselves, after removing their clothing. Cold water stung, yet refreshed and clouds of yellow-gray grime floated away from them. Joey touched himself gingerly, then rose above the water. Their crotches were inflamed and reddened from the rock dust.

Their feet had suffered also. When they completed their bathing, Joey went to Mule-Ear. "Mister Johnson, could we have some boots? And some loose pants to wear. All that fine grit is rubbin' us sore down here," he explained, gripping his crotch.

"Well now, things like that cost money," Johnson began.

"We won't be able to work for long if we keep getting rubbed raw where our legs come together. What good are we like that?"

"Ummmm. You've a good point, Joey, lad. I'll see to it. Now eat up and turn in. Nights are still mighty cool."

Three nights later, still smarting and burning from the irritation of the sharp-edged particles, the boys lay tied in their bonds. *Pangeca,* whose name meant Person with Unusual Talents, began to wriggle with as much silence as he could manage. Since early childhood, his limp, elastic joints enabled him to twist and turn, and most importantly, to manage to escape from any sort of restraints placed on him. Johnson had not as yet produced the badly needed clothing and the youngsters had decided they had to make an escape before their condition grew any worse. After the white miners had turned in, Joey gave the go-ahead to *Pangeca.*

Now the Oglala boy rolled onto his belly, wiggled a bit more and sigh exploded through his nose. "I'm free," he informed his friends in a whisper.

"Untie Badger next," Joey hissed.

"No, *Pinspinzala* first," Badger protested.

"Be quiet," Joey urged. "Do Badger."

Swiftly, *Pangeca* undid the leather straps holding *Hka.* Then he turned to Joey and freed him. Joey held a finger over his lips as he rose to a crouch.

"Be quiet," he urged. "Don't wake them."

Moving on tiptoe, the boys made a line due south from the claim. They avoided the horses and mules because of not being familiar with them. Joey estimated they had made a good mile toward where *Mahtolasan* had been left behind when they heard the thud of hoofbeats. At once they scattered, though to no avail.

"I see you there, you heathen bastard," Red Tyback growled. "C'mon out."

Leather creaked, then hissed through the air. Badger cried out as the bullwhip lash cut through the skin of his back. The whip cracked again. Joey bit his lip and listened to his friend's agony. Once more.

"Stop!" Joey called out. "If you stop, we'll all come out."

"Show yourselves, then," Red snarled.

Faces averted, the trio stepped into the moonlight. Tyback dismounted and produced manacles and leg irons. These he fastened to each boy, ignoring the thin streamers of blood running on Badger's back. In the saddle again, Red fell in behind them and started off to the mine. When they reached the camp, the fire had been built up and a kerosene lantern provided added illumination. Tyback quickly lined the youngsters up and stepped behind them.

"I'll learn you to run off on us, by God I will," he shouted.

Twice more the bullwhip slithered through the air and cut into Beaver's back. The boy writhed and grunted, but made no outcry. Then Red laid into *Pangeca*. Five times the lash cut flesh, and tears ran silently. *Pangeca* dropped to his knees after the fifth

61

stripe.

"Now for you. You gotta be the ring-leader, 'cause yer the only one knows what we say or do," Red informed Joey.

He stretched out the whip and brought it forward. Fire exploded across Joey's shoulderblades. He bit so firmly on his lower lip that he drew blood. Still, he hadn't yet cried out or shed a tear. Another bolt of agony cut into him. He shuddered and sighed, and kept his feet. Slowly Joey turned his head to look at the man who brutalized him.

"Mom Becky'll kill you when she finds out," he said coldly. "An' *Tatekohom'ni*'ll take your scalp."

The lash started to move again. "No!" Mule-Ear Johnson shouted. "Don't do it. We'll have to make do without them for a week if you cut 'em up too bad. Let be for now."

"Dang you, Mule-Ear, we gotta learn them a lesson."

"What we gotta do is clean 'em up, bandage those welts and get 'em to bed. A bit of hot stew an' some coffee wouldn't hurt, either. And if you don't want 'em caught up with festerin' and fever, I'd find a better place than the bare ground for 'em to sleep. They need blankets, too."

Red Tyback looked around angrily and settled upon the mine. "I'll chain 'em inside the mine entrance. Keep the dew off an' make it harder to try to escape."

"Whatever," Mule-Ear agreed. "So long as you don't hurt 'em any more."

"You goin' soft on me, Porter?" Red taunted.

"Nope. Only . . . I've got me to thinkin'. Maybe that towheaded wart knows something we don't."

Chapter 6

Early morning sunshine made tiny diamonds of the dewdrops on the tall buffalo grass. Sage, lupine and daisies gave the dawn air a heady richness as Rebecca Caldwell Ridgeway started off on the final day's journey. Funeral services over for Buell Holbert, she had set out promptly to return and take up the search for the missing children. The additional burden of recently losing someone else dear to her sat heavily upon her mind. It certainly did not prepare her for the news she received when she reached the Oglala village at mid-afternoon.

"It's all my fault," Whirlwind said miserably. "I should have been watching closer. *Pinspinzala, Hoka* . . ." he named off the missing children.

Stunned, Rebecca could only stare at him. This new event made her life seem more certainly filled with nothing but tragedy and disaster. *Joey!* Stolen away like the others. *She* should have been there. Her throat constricted and she tried to form words, only to fail.

"I'm not fit to be called a warrior," Whirlwind declared flatly. "I broke my faith with you and let

63

Pinspinzala be stolen away."

"The . . . others who were taken? What of them?" Rebecca heard herself ask.

"Three were friends of your son. The others, boys and girls of the village. They have been gone ten sleeps."

"Didn't anyone go after them? Wasn't something done?" Rebecca demanded, her wretchedness overpowering.

"We searched," Whirlwind admitted. "Many tracks led to the far side of the reservation, in the direction where the sun sleeps. From there, more horses joined. A large party went on that way until they reached hard ground. We lost the trail. There was a creek beyond and we never found any sign of where they might have come out. The mothers already grieved and most spoke for giving up the search. Word will come and we will go for the children, they said."

"I want to see Major Storey," Rebecca decided aloud. "Then you and I will start another search. From what you say, there must be some sort of organization behind this. If so, we will have a hard time freeing the children."

"I'm not worthy. I am no longer a warrior," Whirlwind repeated in resignation.

Compassion flooded Rebecca. "Don't you think I'm hurting inside? Don't you know that I feel responsible? Come with me, Whirlwind. We'll see what can be done."

Whirlwind lowered his head. "I will wait the judgment of my Badger Society brothers. When they have spoken, I'll come to you."

"Whirl—wind," Rebecca began weakly. Then she

turned away and mounted her spotted rump stallion, Śila.

Major Harvey Storey greeted Rebecca and offered an expression of his regret for her unfortunate circumstance. He ushered her into a small parlor off his office and called for coffee. When they had taken seats, he directly addressed the problem.

"What else may I do for you, Mrs. Ridgeway."

"Please, it was Rebecca and Harvey, as I recall," Rebecca opened. "What I need is based on what I intend to do. I'm going after Joey and the other children. Now that there have been definite losses from this agency, you have a certain degree of authority to investigate, is that correct?"

"Yes, it is, Rebecca. Regulations that govern the reservations are uniform. Unfortunately, the size of any given staff is not. I haven't the soldiers, or Indian Police for that matter, to do a great deal more than is currently being done by other agencies."

"I understand that. And I have a proposition for you," Rebecca offered in return.

Harvey Storey raised an eyebrow. "Oh? What may I ask?"

"You haven't but a handful of Indian Police because the Red Top Lodge Oglala don't as yet trust the agency system, am I right, Harvey?"

"You are, Rebecca. 'Though for the life of me, I can't contrive any way to alter that situation."

"I can," Rebecca stated confidently. "Whirlwind, and through him, the entire Badger Society, feels responsible for the abduction of my step-son, and the other children. Particularly those who were with Joey when he disappeared. From past experience with this band, I feel that the *Ihoka* might consider the proper way to proceed is to go hunting the children themselves. If they do, it would facilitate things if you were to draw up papers making them Indian Police. Also to provide me with a letter authorizing me to conduct an investigation on your behalf."

Consternation and dawning admiration expressed themselves on Major Storey's face. "You're asking a lot, Rebecca. 'Though fortunately not more than I can give. I'd feel a mite better if you wouldn't take a personal part in this. Whoever is behind this has to be dangerous."

Rebecca smiled softly. "Not more so than the outlaws I've tracked down in the past, Harvey. I have a friend, a man who has helped me before. He's in the Black Hills now. With him, and Whirlwind's *Ihokapi*, I have no doubt we can be of considerable use in ending all this."

Storey sighed and clapped his hands together. "It will take a day or so. I'll have to have names, descriptions, that sort of thing. When you have that for me, we can get started."

"I should have an answer yet today, Harvey," she informed him, rising to depart.

Near sunset, Whirlwind came to Rebecca's lodge. His presence dispelled the gloom of emptiness. Unaware she had been holding it, Rebecca put aside one of Joey's shirts and made Whirlwind welcome.

In a rush, Whirlwind explained what had occurred

66

in her absence. "My brothers of the *Ihoka* have decided that my shame is their shame. They want to do something to get the missing children back here."

Rebecca smiled. "I thought they might see it that way. Major Storey will put the marks on paper that will make the Badger Society policemen for the agency. As Indian Police, you can leave here armed, seek the children, and not fear the Army."

"Is such a thing possible?" Whirlwind found it hard to believe. They had heard nothing good about the Indian Police program and so distrusted it.

"Of course it is. All Harvey, ah, the major needs are the names of your warrior society members, their descriptions and the weapons they will carry. Then he sets it in words and all must respect your right to go your way." Rebecca found her enthusiasm growing with her explanation.

"We can recover our honor?" Whirlwind said wonderingly.

Rebecca moved closer. "To me, you never lost it."

Tenderly, she touched him on the shoulder, moved her hand lightly up to his cheek. Then she guided his lips to hers. Their kiss lasted a long while, growing in fervor. Whirlwind enfolded Rebecca in his arms.

"I dared not come to you," he breathed softly into one ear.

"Why? My loss has weakened me. I terribly need someone to lean upon. Someone to help me. If . . . if it's someone who can fill my, ah, physical needs as well, I can be whole again. Love me, Whirlwind. Take me as your own and drive away the creatures of darkness that fill my mind," Rebecca pleaded, her passion growing, burning, yet tender.

With matching gentleness, Whirlwind undressed her. Revealed to the firelight, her splendid breasts rose from her thin chest like twin mountains. At the touch of his large thumbs, the nipples tingled and began to firm. Her hands fumbled at his vest and bone breast plate. Breath roughened, she made small grunting sounds as she removed them. She placed her cheek on his hairless chest and listened to the accelerated thumping of his heart.

His eager lips replaced Whirlwind's thumbs and his long, strong fingers continued to explore the contours of her magnificent body, sweeping downward with tantalizing slowness. Rebecca's pulse quickened and her hands sought out his loincloth. She drew it from the wide buckskin sash at his waist and cast the long flap of softened deer hide aside. One palm cupped his aroused flesh and Whirlwind moaned.

"I . . . sometimes after *Pinspinzala* and the others disappeared, I feared we would never make love again," Whirlwind confided.

"You've only awakened me, Whirlwind. I would die without your presence, your support. Th-this is what makes even that more complete."

Whirlwind began to kiss her ardently upon the breasts, her belly and lower.

Slowly they made love. Every care whirled away in the consuming passion of the moment. Lips and tongues blurred with motion, as they delved within and along in ever increasing euphoria. Nerves short-circuited under the load of sensation, and muscles tensed with iron rigidity as they scaled the heights and erupted into completion. Warm juices melted the icy spires of anxiety and concern. Without a moment's respite, they repositioned themselves upon a pile of buffalo robes. At passion's crescendo, Whirlwind entered her, hips driving his potent shaft far within her body.

Little cries of joy escaped Rebecca's straining throat. Moans and grunts of newly approaching completion burst from deep in Whirlwind's chest. Snowshowers of colored petals filled Rebecca's mind, easing all care. A chorus of sweet-voiced flutes sang in Whirlwind's ears, banishing any self-doubt.

With many words and touches, peaked by urgent, compelling coupling, they spent the long night in slow, tender, healing love.

"There it is, Deadwood City," Niel Mallory called out to the members of the *Venganza* gang.

The name had been suggested by Loomis Clutter, who had admitted to "traveling around some in Mexico." It meant *vengeance*, he'd informed the others. It fitted, the newly joined members agreed, so it stuck. Now they had reached their temporary goal and spirits rose.

"How long we gonna stay, Boss?" Paddy O'Toole inquired of Clutter.

Loomis Clutter considered the question a moment and cast a glance to Lane Tulley, whom he had come to respect considerably more over the past two weeks. "Two days," he advised, noting Tulley's nod of approval. "Maybe three. Depends on whether we hear anything on Baylor. If we do, we light a shuck damn' fast."

"Suits," Al Honeycutt stated simply. "I want to wash

the trail dust outta my throat, wet my tallywhacker a bit and get a good meal. After that, I'm for gettin' the hunting out of the way and settle down to make a nice little profit."

"What you mean by that?" Ray Dawson demanded. His close-set black eyes glittered with the same porcine malevolence of his late twin brother, Big Dick. His 197 pounds on a five foot six frame, with moon face and jowls, added to his hoggish appearance.

"We've been doin' all right so far," Al informed him. "So, once we finish off this Lone Wolf and the woman, there's no reason we shouldn't stick together and clean out a few places so's to make our lives comfortable for a while, eh?"

"I ain't in this to be some owlhoot on the run," Ray whined. "We get our paychecks for our kin and break up, I say."

"Well, then, it's a good thing there's some in this outfit with more say than you, ain't it?" Honeycutt drawled.

Snake-quick, Ray Dawson started for the Smith and Wesson American he wore in a high cross-draw rig under his coat. Peter Dillon, son of Opie Dillon, an old-timer with the original gang, whipped a fast hand over and closed it on Ray Dawson's wrist. His large hand squeezed with considerable strength for a youth of seventeen.

"Let's not have any of that," he purred quietly.

"Why'dn't we stop this jawin' and ride on in?" Paddy O'Toole inquired. "I'm gettin' a powerful thirst and a rail-stiff pecker."

"Now, those are the first intelligent words I've heard since we reined in," Al Honeycutt said lightly, his icy, nearly colorless blue eyes fixed on Ray Dawson.

Half an hour later, his belly filled with bear steak, potatoes and six eggs, a dollar's worth of two-bit whiskey under his belt, Paddy O'Toole rolled into Lotta Crabtree's bordello in Deadwood City. Beyond the heavy front door, thick protective curtains and tightly closed windows, the dust of the gulch, acrid wood smoke and smelter odors had been banished. All Paddy could smell was the closeness of female bodies.

Their mere presence caused his arousal. Eagerly he looked around him, seeking his preference, while he licked his lips in excellent imitation of a cat dunked in a bowl of cream. Outwardly, the soiled doves of the establishment saw a round-faced, pug nosed, pleasant appearing young man with curly black hair, a protruding belly and an obvious erection. What they couldn't see was the other hereditary endowments of the O'Toole clan.

Although not so dull-witted as his uncle, Bobby O'Toole, eighteen year old Patrick had also been cursed with below average intelligence. He likewise shared his infamous uncle's preoccupation with torturing small animals and his lust for sexually abusing females. Tonight he hoped to find release, but without resorting to bloodshed.

"Are you looking for someone in particular, handsome?" a frizzy-haired blonde inquired, brushing her firm bosom against Paddy's chest.

"Gah-unng! Er, ah, n-no. Not anyone by name. I'm new here," Paddy managed to get out.

"I'm Giselle. What's your name?"

"Gaw-er—ah, Patrick. P-Paddy, my friends call me."

71

"Well then, Paddy, would you buy a lady a drink? That way we could introduce you around and you'd not be a stranger."

"Oh, ah, sure, sure. What would you like?" Paddy croaked from a dry throat. He'd seen several young lovelies, any of which might inspire him to an explosive climax, giving the proper circumstances.

"Can you afford champagne, Paddy?"

"Yep. I got a whole pocket full of double eagles," Paddy bragged, unable to register the danger of being too open about such matters in a place of this nature.

"Then champagne it is. Set 'em up, Sam," she called to the apron.

The barkeep arrived with two stemmed glasses and a chilled bottle of bubbly. He unwound the wire retainer and used two thumbs to pop the cork. While it still foamed, he deftly dispensed two portions and set the towel-wrapped remainder before Paddy. Paddy and Giselle clinked rims and sipped the sparkling wine with true appreciation. To the youthful outlaw it tasted sublime. Twenty minutes passed in idle chatter. Then Paddy's knees went limp and he thought his heart would leap from his chest.

Through the mirror behind the bar he saw a small, curvaceous, dusky-skinned girl descend beside another girl and what must be her latest customer. She had a heart-shaped face, coppery complexion, big, sad black eyes and a pleasing mouth. Tiny breasts, hardly formed, protruded behind a wide, lawn lace filler in the bodice of her short, frilly bar dress.

"Oh, my God, I'm in love," he panted weakly.

Giselle saw the direction of his attention and produced a resigned smile. Lately so many miners, it

72

seemed, lusted after the young ones. It must have something to do with their origins in the hills of Appalachia and the Blue Ridge. A gambler had once told her that among the hill people, girls were darned near all sexually active at seven or eight and married by eleven. A child of twelve or thirteen who hadn't borne one or more children herself, to one or more husbands, was considered an old maid. And here she hadn't even started the shyest sort of fooling around until after she'd reached fourteen, Giselle considered. Here stood another one, she accepted unhappily. Could it be possible to be too old for the business at the tender age of nineteen?

"Oh, you mean North Star?" Giselle put a good face on it. "That's what we call her. She's new here. Sort of an apprentice. She don't now all the ways to thrill a man that the rest of us do. So we usually work in tandem."

"Right now, I don't mind at all. Nosiree, not at all. You'll forgive me, Giselle? When I'm done, I promise I'll come back to you."

So saying, Paddy O'Toole started off toward the little Indian girl. The high quality Meierhoff razor burned hotly in its soft leather pouch between his shoulderblades.

Chapter 7

Smoke rose from a dozen festive cookfires, sending sparks into the darkness, orange messengers amid disappearing twists of smoke. Rich aromas from dog stew and fresh roasting buffalo filled the night air. Mounted on a shaggy, whorl-haired pony, wearing the paraphernalia of an *Eyanpaha*, the chief of the Badger Society rode through the rings of the Red Top village, a many-feathered lance in one hand, a black-stemmed pipe, with red feathers trailing, resting in the crook of his other arm.

"I am *Nugepitanka*, Chief of the *Ihoka!* I carry the pipe of war! Who among the Badger Society will come and touch the pipe? We take the war trail against the child stealers. Who will touch the pipe?"

Drums began to throb and old voices rose in a chant, telling of the bravery of the Badger Society. Small boys ran shrilly through the village on stick horses, making mock war of their own. Older lads, of ten to fourteen, felt the tug at their hearts and the quickening of their blood. Many, too, felt the stirring, stiffening in their loins that called to them to do acts of bravery and manhood. Rebecca stood before her lodge and passed to each warrior who touched the pipe a belt of wampum beads and a stiff fold of paper, declaring them to be Indian Police. In the morning they would receive their blue shell jackets, army kepis, and badges.

They would be armed again. Fighting men with a cause to pursue and an enemy to hunt down. Each of the grinning young men felt like a warrior for the first time since regretfully coming to the agency. That a woman would lead them meant little. Not when that woman was *Šinaskawin,* the White Robe Warrior Woman of their own band. Whirlwind came to stand beside her as she handed out still more of the symbols of authority.

"Are you pleased?" he asked in Lakota.

"Beyond all expectations," Rebecca answered honestly.

"I count four hands of Badgers who have touched the pipe," Whirlwind said proudly.

"Twenty warriors," Rebecca repeated. "With the three of us, we should be able to find what is going on and stop it quickly."

"I would wish it to be a hand times that many," Whirlwind stated. "That way we would ride over these evil men and leave not even a wet smear."

"My, we're blood-thirsty tonight," Rebecca said with a hint of sarcasm.

"I thirst for you. Tonight's our last time for love until after our enemy is vanquished."

"Then we had better make it a good one," Rebecca

urged.

Screams came from behind the heavy blanket that formed a barrier in the doorway of the narrow cubicle. Each was punctuated with a meaty smack of a palm against skin. The first couple went ignored, it was a common enough sound in a brothel like Lotta Crabtree's. The angry male voice that rose a moment later drew more attention.

"I said *suck,* damnit!" Paddy O'Toole snarled. "An' that's what I mean."

"Don't hurt me," a small voice in Lakota pleaded.

O'Toole hit her again. This time he used a closed fist. " 'Smatter? Don't you speak English?"

Hard knuckles cracked into her ribcage again. The tiny, fragile bones snapped and the Sioux girl called North Star by her sister prostitutes shrieked in pain. For the first time, O'Toole's eyes widened in worry. He shook her roughly.

"Be quiet, y'hear? Shut off that noise and suck me."

When she continued to whimper and the tears slid down her cheeks, O'Toole hit her in the face. The sight of blood streaming from her nostrils excited Paddy O'Toole beyond his ability to contain himself. He took her savagely and she cried out in terror.

He thought of the razor and decided to give her another, final try later on. In the next moment, the blanket partition flew aside to reveal a furious Lotta Crabtree.

"What did you do to her, you son of a bitch?" she demanded after a shocked look at the supine Indian child. "You were told she wasn't to be used like that.

76

Goddamn you, now you've ruint her for sure!"

A diminutive .41 rimfire derringer appeared in Lotta's hand. It cracked loudly in the confines of the whorehouse crib. A cottony puff of powder smoke bloomed behind the lance of orange flame. Paddy O'Toole felt a ripple of air and a burning scrape along the skin where his neck joined his shoulder.

"Ow! You got no call to hurt me, lady. I didn't do anything."

"The hell you didn't," Lotta charged, advancing on him to use the other barrel. "Girl cost me a pretty dollar. Now you come in here and near killed her."

"Don't shoot me again, lady, please. Why'd they let me come up here if she wasn't all right for some fun?"

"My overseer thought you were bringing Giselle, too. This one's for hand jobs and such, usually along with another girl. A two on one. You ever try that?"

"Naw. Never considered that before," Paddy admitted. Keep her talking, he thought. Maybe she'd forget about shooting.

Lotta had stepped to the bed and began to examine the sobbing girl. "You bastard, you broke her up mighty awful. I don't abide by no hittin' girls." She turned a hard eye on Paddy. "You bust up valuable property, you've gotta pay for it. One hundred dollars," the last snapped like the closing of a cash drawer.

"I ain't got a hundred dollars to pay for a bit of a thing like her. 'Sides, what would I do with her after?"

"You wouldn't be taking her. I only figured my loss while she recovers," Lotta told him coldly. "If I were to let some of the boys downstairs know about this . . ." she let the threat hang.

Paddy O'Toole began to shrug into his clothing,

drawing on his boots last of all. His dim brain perceived danger readily enough and swirled in an attempt to find a solution. He could come up with only one. Her guard down, Lotta no longer pointed the derringer at him. He took a swift step forward and punched her in the side of the head.

Lotta grunted, sighed and flopped against the bed, her tinted curls resting on the heaving belly of the Sioux girl. Instantly, Paddy made a dash for the door. In the hall he turned to the rear of the building and sprinted noisily toward the stairwell. Boots clumping a rapid tattoo, he lumbered down the steep steps and burst out through a flimsy back door. His lungs bellowed as he churned through the dust, leather soles crunching on broken glass shards.

"Hey, boys!" he began to yell. "Hey, Lane, Ike, Matt! C'mon. We gotta get outta here," his panicked appeal continued, while behind an uproar began in Lotta Crabtree's salon of sin.

Within ten minutes the *Verganza* gang spurred out of Deadwood City. Angry at the stupidity and senseless brutality of Paddy O'Toole, several vowed to settle his hash the moment their search for revenge ended. Sweating from exertion and fear, Paddy O'Toole solemnly swore to himself to make it up to his companions at the first opportunity. Back in Deadwood they left a broken and bleeding Sioux girl and a sore and angrily raving Lotta Crabtree.

Mourning doves still *too-hooted* their solemn lament when the party of twenty-seven Badger Society warriors, led by Rebecca, Whirlwind and Big Ears, rode off from the Rosebud reservation. Several had that logy condition from lack of sleep that resembled the white man's hangover. The dancing and celebration had gone on until far after midnight. Under the warming sun they would pay for it. Their course took them toward the sacred Black Hills. Previous attempts to track the child stealers led in that direction and Rebecca had a strong suspicion that they would at least learn something there. Also, Lone Wolf would be somewhere in those awesome folds and heaves in the prairie. Whirlwind knew Lone Wolf from past times and spoke of him as they cantered along.

"If the children are alive, and in the *hesapa* as you think, Lone Wolf will know of them."

"I'm sure he will. That's why we want to find him first thing," Rebecca agreed. "I've been thinking, too, that if whoever took them didn't simply want to kill the children, where could they be taken to make some profit from selling them? The Black Hills seem to fit."

"How is that?" Whirlwind inquired.

"I'm not certain yet. We'll learn more when we get there."

A little more than half way to their goal, an advance scout rode back to hail the column of warriors. "A white man comes this way. He has long, white hair on his chin. He rides a long-ear and leads two more. We do not know him."

Rebecca considered this terse report. "I think you and I should ride forward and talk with him. It would be better than coming at him with so many warriors," she suggested to Whirlwind.

He readily agreed and they started off, after Big Ear gave the command to halt the cavalcade. Over a

79

grassy knoll, shimmering green in the sun, they trotted down toward a faint trail. Plodding along it came a bent-back old man, a floppy, weathered hat drooping around his head. He rode a mule and led two more. Picks, shovels and a gold pan could be seen on the outside of one large pack rig. Rebecca hailed him in English from a distance.

"Eh?" came the faint reply. "Devil take me, ya look like savages, but you talk straight enough. C'mon down."

When Rebecca and Whirlwind joined him, he studied them, hands on hips, eyes glittering from a nest of wrinkles. At last satisfied, he stuck out a hard, callused hand. "M'name's Jake Naylor. Went bust prospectin' in the Hills and decided to light out."

"Rebecca Ridgeway," the white squaw responded. "This is Whirlwind. He speaks enough English to understand if you don't talk too fast."

Naylor cocked his head to one side. "He your man?"

"Not exactly. We're, ah, friends. I live on the Rosebud Agency with my son, Joey Ridgeway. That's a long story for another time," she dismissed. "We're on our way to the Black Hills. Someone has been stealing children from all of the reservations. Sioux and Cheyenne boys and girls of about ten to fourteen years in age. We have a detail of Indian Police with us to search out information. Do you happen to know anything that might be useful to us?"

Jake Naylor pondered a moment. "Feller hears a lot of things, ain't al'ays true. There's talk of slaves bein' used in the bigger mines. Never saw anything like. Trust my own eyes, that's my motto. What I did see is

80

a pair of little Sioux girls being manhandled through the back door of a bawdy house in Alder Gulch back a couple of weeks. They'd be about the size you was sayin'."

"You're sure of this?" Rebecca prompted.

"Saw it personal-like, Miss. That I can say for sure. Don't cotton to those who'd make use of little ones like that. Might be you want to start off lookin' there."

"Which place?" Rebecca urged. "Do you recall the name of the establishment, Mister Naylor?"

"Ummm. Don't read all that well. I think it was called Lotta's Re-something or other Rest."

"Thank you so much, Mister Naylor," Rebecca responded sincerely. "I'm sure we can find it from that. I particularly appreciate your help, since my step-son is one of the missing."

"Be danged. Shore are sorry to hear that, Miss. You all take care and good luck findin' the lost tads."

Naylor started off and Whirlwind gave out an excellent imitation of a coyote howl. Within seconds the newly appointed Indian Police rode over the rise. Naylor glanced their way and his startled remarks carried to Rebecca's ears on the still prairie air.

"Lord a Goshen, a feller'd think the Sioux Wars was goin' again."

Alder Gulch enjoyed a lesser popularity to the larger Deadwood City, premier boomtown of the Black Hills. All along the wide floodplain of the broad notch, mining activity flourished. As more gold seekers arrived the small camps spread out, threatening to join into one huge, long community. Fires had swept

81

through often, reducing parts of the tent and timber towns to blackened rubble. Always the lust for the yellow metal had built them up again. Few Indians visited the place, the population being almost evenly divided between Irish Catholics and Scots Protestants.

Both Deadwood and Alder Gulch boasted a miner's hall, each of which had been laid out according to certain honored principles and contained the paraphernalia of an order that traced its origins back to ancient Egypt. The communities also had tiny chapels, presided over by priests of the Dominican Fathers. In spite of this, saloons and brothels far outnumbered any other form of enterprise. With these facts in mind, Rebecca wisely halted their force at some distance. There she changed into her modern clothing and admonished the Oglala police to remain well out of sight. Riding alone, she started for Alder Gulch.

Rebecca covered little territory before her presence became known. Friendly hails and waves came from hard-bitten miners working their claims, often wet to their waists, or covered with the dust of digging the mountain side. An occasional low, appreciative whistle sounded from the less conventional, or bolder of the workers. A haze of blue-white smoke rose in the distance, marking the location of the mining camp. Half an hour's ride brought her to where she could see the outline of peaked tents and an occasional wooden building. Urging more speed from *Śila*, Rebecca cantered over a fold of the canyon and downslope toward the spreading vista of Alder Gulch.

"Yer new around these parts, pretty lady," a well inebriated miner slured as Rebecca nosed her Palouse horse along the wide, muddy single street of Alder Gulch.

Rebecca ignored him, and the salutations of other celebrants in the streets. Her destination, the largest bordello in town, lay at some distance. From off in side canyons came the infrequent dull boom and rumble of explosive charges detonating to crack rock and force the ancient hills to give up their precious treasure. A block short of her goal, two tall, lean men in faded Army shell jackets and kepis attracted her attention.

One of them had gestured from the mouth of an alley. The flicker of movement registered on her cautious observation and she reined in. It took only a moment to recognize the older of the pair. Stone Breaker, a Crow friend of Lone Wolf, who had long served for the Army as a contract scout. His familiar features helped her to quickly identify his companion. Two Owls. Lone Wolf had spoken of him often. Another scout, he carried himself with a certain air that was not wholly Indian, nor white. Pleased, she waved to them and guided *Sila* to a tie-rail beside the short opening between buildings.

"Stone Breaker, Two Owls, I'm pleased to see you here," she greeted.

"I almost didn't recognize you, dressed like that," Stone Breaker admitted in excellent English.

"I thought it best, ah, considering the mood around here," she responded, wondering why she needed to explain at all.

"We've only been discharged from the scout company. The men here know we have worked for the troops to keep the hostiles from raiding, so we are, ah, tolerated," Stone Breaker replied. "Though we must make our purchases from the back door."

Rebecca detected more of a note of contempt than bitterness in Stone Breaker's words. It somehow pleased her. Spirits lifted, she proceeded lightly with small-talk. "What brings you here, then?"

"We needed supplies. Two Owls and I are searching for Lone Wolf," came Stone Breaker's answer.

"He's fasting and praying to climb to the Power Road," Rebecca responded.

"So we have heard from our relatives in our home village," Two Owls remarked. "He has completed his spirit voyage and been elevated to that place known as Spirit Talker among medicine men. Yet he is in grave danger. During our last days with the Army, we heard words of importance to our brother Lone Wolf."

At once concerned, Rebecca produced a slight frown. "What's this about?"

Stone Breaker took up the tale. "He is being hunted by a large band of white men. Many are from the families of the outlaws who rode with Jake Tulley. The danger Two Owls spoke of extends also to you, *Sinaskawin,* our Oglala friend. These men intend to find Lone Wolf and you and kill the both of you."

Chapter 8

"Lotta, we've got trouble," a worried prostitute announced as she entered Lotta Crabtree's office in the Deadwood City bordello. Eyes red from weeping, she stood twisting her fingers together.

"What is it, Clara?"

"Th-that, ah, North Star's died, Lotta. I went to give her some soup and she was lying there on the bed, not breathin', and all still."

"Damn! And damn that stupid drifter son of a bitch who messed her up like that. Well, we'll have to do something about it."

"Fetch the undertaker?" Clara suggested.

"No, damnit. We'd wind up with the blame. What we do is bury her ourselves."

Clara paled and began to tremble. "Oh, oh, Lotta, we couldn't do a thing like that. No proper Christian burial and such."

"She was a heathen," Lotta hissed. "Don't forget

85

that. Also I bought an' paid for her, which makes her a slave in a country that's outlawed slavery. Get Tobias and Sammy and have them dig a hole out in No Color Draw. We'll wrap her in a blanket later on and go out after things quiet down."

Sniffling, Clara started for the door. "It all seems so cold and — and uncaring."

"You think I don't care? Goddamnit, I care one whole lot. Look at the money I invested and now've lost thanks to that damned animal and his sick ways."

Nothing ever stopped in Deadwood. Some establishments closed for a few hours, their services being provided by another just opening. Meals were served around the clock, whiskey dispensed endlessly, girls available at any hour, games of chance or tools could be had any time. Yet in the small hours of the morning, around two or three, business slacked off. At two-thirty, a converted buckboard — a buggy top fitted over the high, spring-mounted seat — pulled up to the back of Lotta Crabtree's house of ill-repute.

Silently, two men loaded a small, light bundle into the wagon box and climbed in after. Lotta and two of her girls mounted the wheel to the seat. There they situated themselves and Lotta lightly slapped the reins on the rumps of the team. Without conversation, they rolled out of Deadwood, toward the emptiness called No Color Draw, one of the few places gold had not been discovered among the rich deposits of the Black Hills. Three miles from town, the buckboard stopped.

"There it is, Miss Lotta," Tobias spoke in a whisper.

"Get her out, then, Toby. Then you an' Sam follow me over to the gr — ah, place."

"Miss Lotta, I don't zactly like this," Tobias appealed, rolling big marble-sized whites in their ebon-surrounded sockets. "We's like as sure to get the hants after us."

"Oh nonsense," Lotta snapped. "To the devil with your Gullah superstitions. All that is is a body. Dump it in the ground like a side of meat gone bad and forget it. Nothing will happen."

"Lawdie, Miss Lotta, y'all sure on that? Seems . . ."

"Be quiet," Lotta hissed. "Do as I say, or do you want me to turn you out in the streets? A number of those Southern boys in the mining camps just might find some white robes and pointy hats in their personals bags."

Tobias fairly trembled. "Aw, naw, Miss Lotta. Don' go talkin any of that *klu kluxin'* around like that, please."

"Then be quick about it and let's get out of here."

For all her impatience at the bordello's handyman, Lotta also felt a strange stirring, as though the night and all the things it hid conspired against her. She would, she decided, have a good stiff shot of brandy once they returned to town. Perhaps it would help in putting her to sleep. Unspeaking, she lined up with the two soiled doves, beside the open grave. Overhead, in the branches of a softly moaning pine, an owl hooted interrogatively.

"Oh, Lawd, I done said the hants was gonna come fo' us," Tobias moaned.

"Shut! Up! Tobias," Lotta blurted, herself unnerved by the unexpected sound.

Nervous hands released the blanket prematurely. The shrouded body made a solid thump in the bottom of the grave. Lotta stepped close and peered into the

87

sooty interior.

"Ashes to ashes, and dust to dust," she sighed out. "So long, Honey. Too bad you had to die so young. But then, maybe Injun girls are more fragile that others."

"May I say something?" Clara appealed.

"Go on," Lotta snapped, eager to get away from this eerie scene.

"Lord Jesus, please accept the soul of this poor, lost thing. I know she was a savage and a heathen," Clara said softly, eyes upturned to the heavens. "But she's so tiny and alone. I guess that's all. A-men."

"Fill it in and let's get out of here," Lotta commanded urgently.

Caught in the talons of a hunting nighthawk, a small rabbit squealed pitifully, the cry of an anguished child, from far away. Lotta shivered in sudden, unavoidable fear of the supernatural.

Rebecca had returned to the war camp from Alder Gulch without verifying the presence of Sioux girls in the bordello. Her feelings split three ways, Rebecca found herself in an awful quandary. Whirlwind and his friend, Big Ears, suggested they go to Lone Wolf's aid first. "He is a brother warrior," they said simply.

Rebecca agreed. Yet she felt terrible urgency about locating Joey before any lasting harm came to the boy. It was, after all, her ultimate responsibility. She also ached over the plight of the other Sioux children. Their weighty discussion of alternatives led her to the idea of a compromise.

"Why can't we do this?" she inquired. "I'll return to

Alder Gulch and verify the story of the Sioux girls in the bawdy house. Knowing where we can find some, at least, of the stolen children, we can then hunt for Lone Wolf and have him join us, as planned. Once we're in a position to do so, we can come after the girls and perhaps learn from them where some of the boys have been taken."

Big Ears thought on it through a long silence. Whirlwind nodded ready agreement. Two Owls and Stone Breaker, who had come with her, held out for seeking their adoptive brother Crow, Lone Wolf. Rebecca sensed an impasse developing. She looked from one expressionless, copper face to the other for support. At last, Big Ears spoke.

"Lone Wolf must be helped. Yet the time spent in seeking him leaves the children in great danger. Let these . . ." Big Ears struggled to keep the suppressed hatred of a traditional enemy from showing in his words. *"Abasa* warriors go in search of Lone Wolf, taking any who wish to accompany them. The rest will wait while *Sinaskawin* visits the white village."

Approval quickly went the rounds. Relieved, Rebecca experienced considerable puzzlement when Whirlwind made a covert sign for her to follow him from the council fire. He led her to a secluded spot on a hill. Pine boughs had been cut and laid out to form a comfortable pallet. Over this, Whirlwind had spread several blankets. He drew her close and smiled shyly.

"We're not truly on the war path until we start after the men seeking Lone Wolf, or follow the trail of the child stealers. Which means we have one more night at least, to . . . ah . . ." he hesitantly put forward.

How sweet of him, Rebecca considered. For the sake

89

of his feelings, she made an effort to clarify her attitude. "Many times, when I hunted the Tulley gang," she began, stepping closer, "I didn't abide by the requirements of an Oglala warrior's medicine. If I felt a strong urge for a man, I let my body make the rules. It never lessened my power as a warrior." Quickly she added, "I don't say this to lead you from your beliefs. Only that . . ." Her hand stole to Whirlwind's chest, worked downward. "I understand and agree."

Whirlwind sighed heavily. His left hand cupped one firm globe of a breast and Rebecca murmured softly, deep in her throat. Rebecca lowered her fingers until they teased the sash that held up Whirlwind's loincloth. Tauntingly, she worked her way behind it and delved deeper into his secret place. She found him hotly and rigidly ready.

Below that night-chill surface, mighty fires of passion raged. He pressed his lips to hers. Their tongues probed in darting explorations. Rebecca's natural ability at love-making came to the fore. When their embrace ended, it took little time for them to remove their clothes. Eyes locked in an ardent gaze, they sank slowly to the padded boughs.

Rebecca pressed Whirlwind backward with both hands to his shoulders. Then she straddled him and slowly lowered herself. With a rush of sheer ecstasy, she received him. A faint smile on her lips, Rebecca controlled the entry in such a way as to provide maximum pleasure for both of them. Whirlwind sighed, suddenly uneasy.

"What will come of this?" he inquired in a whisper.

"More happiness than we've ever known," Rebecca

breathed out as she accepted the remainder of his manhood in a single, mighty thrust.

Little sunlight filtered through the thick stand of slender lodgepole pine. Fringing the sinuous slash of forest, mountain laurel gave off a delightfully sweet scent from a plethora of purple blossoms. Birds and small animals had ceased their usual chorus, silenced by the presence of the alien forms of many men. Only the ever-present insects kept up a constant hum and buzz as Lone Wolf Baylor slipped quietly through the stand of pines.

Lone Wolf's destination was a point somewhere behind a group of seven men who noisily and inexpertly pursued him. He had deliberately led them into the thicket, confident in his skills to slip away. When he overheard their remarks regarding killing him and Rebecca Ridgeway, nee Caldwell, it had changed his plans. The hunted became the hunter.

"Over there, 'Lige," a voice drifted back to Lone Wolf's sensitive ears. "He went that way."

"No, Obie, that ain't it at all. See those bent twigs? He went off to the left."

Lone Wolf held his position, letting the searchers draw a bit further away. When the stomping of their boots and crashes of brush faded slightly, he set off after them. The irregular, uphill course he had set for them to follow took a toll on men unaccustomed to such exertions. Within five minutes, they had strung out in an staggered line, two shoulder-to-shoulder, the rest strung out behind. A cold, humorless smile creased the thick lips of the blond warrior and he unsheathed his long fighting knife.

Swift and silent, the long, lean figure closed on the rearmost of the self-appointed posse. A moment before his presence would have been detected, Lone Wolf looped a long arm around the throat of his enemy and drove the knife deep into his back, severely damaging a kidney.

Blood gushed hot and slick over his hand and forearm as Lone Wolf extracted the knife and plunged it again into the small of the back to destroy the man's other kidney. The dying hunter thrashed a moment, then went slack. Lone Wolf eased him to the ground, wiped off his hands, and started after the next.

Obie Dunnem heard a fallen twig crackle behind him. "That you, Harper?" he called out a moment before a large hand clapped over his mouth. Obie tried to scream, even after it was too late.

An icy line of half-felt pain began under his left ear and continued around to the right. A trail of fire followed it as a froth of blood bubbled from his slashed larynx. One moment of clarity let him realize in utter horror that his throat had been slit even as his very soul rushed through the gaping wound. Lone Wolf released his latest victim and moved on for another. He daren't risk an arrow shot; the resultant scream would alert the remaining four. Legs churning with the effort of making a silent, uphill approach, he closed with his enemy.

Once more the Green River trade knife flashed. Buried between a collar bone and shoulder blade, the keen steel cut through the artery and lacerated flesh as the *Venganza* gang member sped off to meet his maker. Once he had the body eased to the ground, Lone

Wolf considered his task complete. With even greater effort at silence, he faded away into the forest.

"Red, we gotta talk this out. This keepin' slaves is gettin' to me," Mule-Ear Johnson stated flatly to his partner.

Red Tyback glanced up from the covered skillet of cornbread he held ready to put in the coals. "What the hell's got into you? Neither of us can get more'n half way back in the digs since a week ago. Them little bitty boys are bringin' out the gold, right enough, but they ain't much on tunneling. We can't blast behind them, it'd squash 'em like bugs. If we stop their work, we stop our makin' that glory hole pay." Tyback gave an elaborate shrug.

"But it ain't right. Even Injun kids has a right to be free," Mule-Ear protested.

"What says?" Red challenged, hands on hips. "The war was fought to free the niggers. *Red* niggers ain't a part of that, I say."

"I wonder what a court would say? Way I hear, there ain't more'n a dozen of us buyin' these kids. Nobody's sayin' a thing. You want to know why? Because they know it's again' the law, that's why."

Tyback squatted again to set a pot of venison stew on the tripod over the coals. "You worry too much, Mule-Ear."

"Them two Oglala boys is takin' on sickly like. I always heard Injuns made poor slaves. Maybe we oughtta treat 'em kinder," Johnson suggested.

"An' do what? Give 'em a share with us in the gold?" Tyback sneered. He rubbed his hands in his faded scarlet beard and cocked his head to one side. "Speakin' of which, grub's gonna be ready in half an hour. What say we eat up, chain them boys and head into town to back our profits? Then maybe we can have a little celebration?"

Mule-Ear glowered a moment, scratched at something crawling in his mustache, and shook his head impatiently. "All right, Red. Only we best provide for the yonkers. Leave 'em plenty food by so they can eat while we're gone."

"Oh, Lord, Mule-Ear, you're worse than my old nigger mammy when I was a little tyke in Geo'gia."

Two hours later, washed, hair and beards trimmed, and spiffed out in clean clothes, Red Tyback and Mule-Ear Johnson presented themselves, grinning impishly, on the porch of Lotta Crabtree's house of sin in Alder Gulch.

Chapter 9

Tinkling strains of a popular favorite drifted from the large main parlor of Lotta Crabtree's Alder Gulch bordello. With a quarter moon and light overcast, only the fitful fires of mine camps and occasional kerosene lanterns illuminated the area. Street lamps were a luxury not as yet required by the rude community. While the festivities progressed within the saloons and pleasure palaces of Alder Gulch, Rebecca Caldwell silently worked her way to the rear of Lotta's establishment.

Dogs barked near and from afar, at real and imagined objects, as the white squaw hugged the shadows of buildings. She reached her goal in time to squeeze back in a pool of blackness while a man staggered out the rear door and made his unsteady way to the outhouse some thirty yards beyond the brothel. Once he closed the chicksale door, Rebecca hurried to the open portal and slipped inside the bawdy house.

She had made twenty feet toward a staircase when a voice further along the hallway stopped her. "You're new around here, ain't ya, Honey?"

"Oh, ah, yes," Rebecca improvised. "I had to, ah, go out back."

A fadingly attractive woman in her mid-twenties advanced into the reflector light of a coal oil lamp. "Don't let Lotta catch you doing that during business hours. Yer supposed to use the thunder mug in your crib."

"Ah, sorry. I'll remember that. And . . . thanks." Rebecca started up the stairway.

"Another thing, Honey. You're a little over-dressed. Get yerself some more feathers and a shorter skirt."

"Sure, sure. First chance I get. Which means soon's I can earn some money."

In the dim light of the upper hallway, Rebecca heaved a sigh of relief. Now she had to find a place from which she could observe all of the inmates of the bordello. Talking openly with them would prove too risky, she considered. On tiptoe, Rebecca progressed along the corridor. She paused to listen at each door. Behind most, she recognized the familiar creak and bump of a bed in passionate use and the moans of the participants. Near the end, she came upon a room that issued forth only light, forlorn sobs.

Tense and watchful, Rebecca continued to listen. Gradually she distinguished two separate vocal tones. Both were light, breathy, like that of a child. Her hopes soared. Bending her lips close, she spoke softly in Lakota.

"*Dakota wayo?*" she asked. A startled gasp sounded inside the small room.

"Ni Dakota wayapi," came a treble reply.

We are Sioux girls! Rebecca's heart swelled. She had been right. Impulsively she reached out to the doorknob. It turned freely but the door failed to open. A caselock. Rebecca fumbled in her hair for a stout pin. When she located it, she bent it into a hook form and inserted it in the cast iron case. A little judicious wiggling and she heard the tumblers engage. From her small reticule she produced a slim-bladed knife and applied tension, then twisted. The lock grated back. An instant later she stood inside, confronted by two thin, naked, thoroughly frightened Sioux girls. Neither could be over fourteen.

Quickly Rebecca explained who she was and her reason for being there. Their previous sobs of despair turned to tears of joy. Would she take them with her right now?

"No. I'm sorry, but I cannot," Rebecca regretfully informed them. "I have friends outside of town. Oglala Indian Police from the Rosebud Agency. We came looking for you and some missing boys. Do you know anything about them?"

"I am called *Kiwani*," the older girl replied. "When we were taken from our homes, some boys were brought along. Some men who dig in the ground gave the yellow metal for those boys who were left with them."

New anger darkened Rebecca's face. "I'll come back. I promise you that. When I do, my friends and I will free you. Keep your hope high."

The smaller girl began to cry. "They make us . . . make us do awful things. When we tried to run away, the big woman who is chief struck us with a riding quirt and took our clothes away. Please make it so we don't have to do those things again."

Sadness, mingled with anger, filled Rebecca's cobalt eyes. She could well picture what the Sioux child meant. Such things should be fun. Had always been fun for her. Sex should be anticipated, enjoyed, not feared and loathed. Damn to hell anyone who would rob these children of that joy. Rebecca reached out and placed a hand on the wide-eyed child's head, drew her close.

"I — I'm sorry that I can't promise you that, little one." She stroked the black tresses with tenderness. "Try anything you can to avoid what they want. It will only be a matter of days. Then I'll come back and you'll be free."

Unable to offer more, and too vulnerable to their anguish, Rebecca started for the door. There she paused and looked back. "I'll have to lock you in, *Kiwani,*" she said apologetically. "Otherwise someone will suspect."

Girding herself against their expressions of desolation she left the room and reset the lock. She had only risen from her effort when a door opened and a bent-shouldered man of middle age, with graying red hair and a tobacco-stained beard of faded scarlet stepped out of another cubicle and stared boldly at her breasts. His pale blue eye was a window, through which Rebecca saw him undressing her in his mind. The other was covered with a greasy black patch.

"Sa-ay, li'l gal. I didn't see you earlier. Lord A'mighty I only just got done with one of your sisters, but lookin' at you's got my pecker ta standin' up right smart again. What'd it take to carry you off to your crib, sweet thing?"

"More than you've got, buster," Rebecca informed him icily.

"They call me Red Tyback, 'cause of my hair and my quick temper. Don't go to rilin' me, Sister, or you might be the sorry one." Tyback made a grab for Rebecca's arm, missed and stumbled into the wainscoted wall. "Com'ere, ya little vixen."

"I told you I'm not available," Rebecca said tightly.

"Yer gonna make yerself available, or Lotta'll hear about this," Red snarled, his mood turning vicious.

"I don't work here, so Lotta's no threat to me," Rebecca stated frostily.

"If you don' work here, what . . . what are you doin' up here?" Fuzzily, Tyback began to suspect something was not as it appeared.

Before his whiskey- and sex-befuddled brain could react to this suspicion, Rebecca reached into her reticule and brought out her .38 Baby Russian revolver. The nickel plating of the Smith and Wesson glittered in the yellow light of the shaded hall lamps. With a sure, solid movement, she shoved it against the side of Tyback's head.

"Before you carry that thought further, I'd suggest you considered how long a time you'd have to spend being dead." The hammer of the S&W .38 clicked to full cock with an ominous sound. "You and I are going to walk quietly down this hall, down the stairs and out the back like old, dear friends. If anyone stops us, or interferes, you die first. Is that clear?"

"Yaunnng!" Red gaped. "Y-you really mean that, don't you?"

"I learned young, never pull a gun on someone

99

unless you have every intention of using it. Now, before your knees give way, and you wet your drawers, let's get going. I'll have the gun inside my reticule, aimed at the middle of your back."

Four frightened members of the *Venganza* gang bore the bodies of their fallen comrades to a small Territory town near the Wyoming border. They had no doubt as to how the trio had died. Lone Wolf Baylor was on the move, headed toward Crow country to the west. He had led them into a trap. Such a defeat smarted heavily and they provided a highly colorful version of events to the law and the local newspaper editor. These tasks completed, they retired to the nearest saloon to wash away the cold, cold fear that clutched their bellies.

"I say we give it up," Peter Dillon, a short, baby-faced killer of only seventeen years announced. "My God, seven of us and that bastard killed near half of us without making a sound."

"Nobody quits until we finish what we came to do," Matt Wellington growled. He took a pull on his glass of whiskey, swiped across his mouth with a hairy hand and glowered at the dissenter. "You plumb yellow to the core? Baylor tricked us, that's all. Next time, we pick the place. That'll be the end of him."

"You're so sure, huh?" Peter Dillon sneered. "When my paw rode with Jake Tulley, no one was ever so sure about anything. Not even Big Jake himself. Especially after this damned Caldwell woman and Baylor started in after them."

"I still say you're yellow. Look at you, a punk kid.

You're so green, you probably think a blow-job is dynamitin' a safe," Wellington goaded.

Peter's face flushed a deep crimson. He came to his feet so rapidly he knocked over the chair. It made a dull thump in the thick sawdust coating of the rough plank floor. Lips curled in sullen anger, his words came in an embarrassingly high pitch.

"Oh, yeah? I'll bet I've got it a lot more than you. I'm gettin' sick of all this talk. I'm goin' out for some air."

With a cocky stride, Dillon sauntered to the batwings. These he pushed aside with enough energy to leave a violent flapping behind. Who the hell did that Matt Wellington think he was? Filled with self-righteous anger, Peter asked himself this question several times. Talkin' about . . . about messin' around like that, out in the open. *Didn't he know?*

Or maybe he did know, another cold thought struck Peter. What if Matt knew all about his past? He'd been only a boy when his father had been killed. Twelve years old. He loved his father, worshipped him in fact. Small wonder his father stayed away from home. Who could possibly love that fat bitch of a wife? Peter's mother. God, how he hated being associated with *her*. It had to be her fault he was such a runt. His dad had been tall, six feet at least. Peter barely topped five foot four. And hardly ninety pounds soaking wet. *She* caused that. Gobbled everything that came into the house. Just the scraps and trims for him and his sisters. She had one thing, though. She was in touch with Jesus. Always praying, shouting around the house, reading her Bible.

Some of it, Peter had to admit, rubbed off on him.

Like about doing dirty things. *She* blamed his failings on his father. Well, maybe that was so. Peter recalled from earliest childhood, for as long as he could remember, that his penis was always erect. Whenever his father would notice the bulge in his trousers, or see him naked, he'd point and holler and say, "Randy little devil, ain't he? Takes after his paw!" By about five or so, when he became aware of the meaning, it embarrassed Peter. With his mother shouting out her holiness all the time, he came to the point where he wanted to cut that offending thing off.

By seven, *she* had taken to accusing him of un-wholesome thoughts and deeds, though in truth he didn't know what that meant. A short while later, a bit of daring experimentation with a friend gave him an idea what that might be. The thing was, if the secret, solitary practice he indulged in late in the night was the "unwholesome" something his mother accused him of, why did it feel so good? That one he never quite reconciled.

In another year, he had made the connection be-tween what animals did together and the source of the remarkable pleasure he generated for himself. If for one it could be fun, his reasoning rapidly concluded, two or more could be so much better. By careful inveigling, Peter managed to induce his friend of past confidences and a little girl from down the street into a game of "Show and Tell," which quickly became "Show and Tickle."

Over the next two years, their mutual entertain-ment grew more sophisticated, while at home, Peter's temper grew to monumental proportions. He often went into rages that ended with him face-down on the

102

floor, breathless and incoherent, his face the ruddy hue of a beet, a froth of spittle at the corners of his mouth. These encounters terrified his mother, who spoke darkly of "possession," and of "driving out the devil."

Such things troubled Peter all the more. A sensitive child, his sandy-blond hair of an exceptionally fine texture, silky skin smooth and sallow, with large, wide-set, deep blue eyes, he felt drawn more and more into the unhealthy world he had created with his friends. When at last their indiscretions resulted in Peter's mother discovering their afternoon activities in the loft above the family stable, Peter received the beating of his life.

His bruises lasted three weeks, at least one rib had been cracked by the savage administration of a broom handle, and he found himself alone, exiled to his room when not doing chores or in school, deprived of contact with any other children. "Child of the devil," his mother muttered darkly. His only companion became the frayed-edged Bible his mother compelled him to read daily. This unnatural and excessive punishment continued until word reached the Dillon home that Opie Dillon, Peter's father, had been killed by a woman named Rebecca Caldwell.

Once again, Peter's rage bloomed malignantly. He attacked his mother in a fury and battered her to the floor. Then he ran from home, weeping wretchedly, his grief driving him to excesses beyond his physical limitations. Sometime during that terrible afternoon, Peter underwent a fateful transition that altered one of the most exquisite experiences of his lustful past into an act of rage.

With utter cunning, he spied out an opportunity to carry off his intention unobserved. Swiftly he seized a seven year old girl from the neighborhood and dragged her off to a secluded spot, where he raped her repeatedly until his fomenting body spent itself and he staggered away to repair the damage to himself and his clothing. The ordeal left his victim mute and the crime was never solved. Within a month, Peter abandoned his home and drifted out west, seeking someone, anyone who had known his father.

His penchant for raping continued. By seventeen, he had tasted of the forbidden fruit more times than he could number. He had the size and sweet, innocent looks of a child of thirteen, something he also blamed on his mother, but inside dwelt a dark entity older than mankind. So let that damned Matt Wellington taunt him, his tormented thoughts summed up. What difference did it make. Peter had become fast and good with a sixgun and rifle and need fear no man. Besides, his achingly swollen penis reminded him, tonight, in this town, would be a good time to hunt.

Chapter 10

Faced into the rising sun, Rebecca Caldwell and her companions pointed their horses to the southwest and worked around the fringes of the Black Hills. Stone Breaker and Two Owls had returned to verify what Rebecca had heard, that Lone Wolf had broken his vigil camp and departed. A cryptic message, in an arrangement of stones and twigs, informed the Crow warriors he intended to make for Crow country.

"With any luck, we should catch up to him in three or four days," Rebecca opined.

"This is the way he said he would go," Stone Breaker insisted. "Signs show no one in his camp for five sleeps. Might be we'll have a long ride ahead of us."

"All the way to Yellow Knife's village?" Rebecca inquired as they rode along at a moderate gait.

"It could be," Stone Breaker acknowledged.

Three days' journey brought them to the small community of Burdock, on the edge of the wild, lonesome Wyoming country. While the entourage made camp outside town, Rebecca rode in to garner any news and for supplies. The local newspaper, displayed in the window of the office, attracted her immediate attention.

WHITE RENEGADE BLAMED IN TRIPLE MURDER!

The large, bold-faced headline glared at her in silent accusation. Somehow she knew it must be Lone Wolf. Worry mounting, she obtained a copy and read into the story. It presented a highly colorful account of an incident in which seven apparently innocent travelers had been attacked by a white renegade and several Indians, three of their party being killed in the resultant fight.

" 'We was up in the Black Hills, movin' west,' " one survivor was quoted. " 'Out of nowhere comes this white man. Only he was dressed like an Indian and he never let out a howdy or nothin', just started in on us.' When asked about the presence of Indians, the man replied, 'That came later, when we tried to escape. These Injuns skulked after us and started killing one by one.' "

That didn't make sense to Rebecca's way of thinking, particularly when the next paragraph named the assailant as Brett Baylor. The man interviewed by the newspaper had to be one of the group of relatives of former Tulley gang members, she reasoned. It might be easier to locate Lone Wolf if she could first locate the men hunting for him and follow them. Toward that end, she turned back to the newspaper office.

"Yes, ma'am?" a pinched face, sallow-complexioned man with green eyeshade and long, black sleeve protectors inquired when Rebecca entered the office.

"I would like to speak to the editor," she requested.

"You're talking to him," came a terse response.

"An article in your latest issue brought me here. The one about a white renegade. Do you happen to have the name of the man you interviewed?"

"Yep. Matter of fact, I do. Let me see now . . ." the editor replied, as he thumbed through a stack of hand-written notes skewered on an iron spike on his desk. "Ah, here it is. Name of Dawson. Raymond Dawson."

"Thank you. What can you recall about him?" Rebecca urged.

"He was short, oh, about five-six or seven, heavy set. Black hair and eyes."

To her discomfort, Rebecca recognized the description as that of Big Dick Dawson, a man she knew she had killed. "Was he, by any chance, left handed?"

"Yes, he was. And always pulling on an earlobe."

Dick Dawson had a nervous habit of pulling his lower lip, Rebecca considered. Could it be a brother? A *twin* brother? "Is Mister Dawson still in town?" Rebecca asked, hopeful her luck hadn't run out.

"As a matter of fact he is. They are. He and his friends are sort of, ah, gathering their strength before heading west again."

"Where could I find him?" Rebecca questioned.

"They're staying at the hotel. Most likely you'll find one or more at the Dutchman. They've been taking on a large load of John Barleycorn since their scrape with the renegade, Baylor. May I ask, what is your interest in this matter, Miss?"

"It's . . . a personal matter. The men listed as killed. One of them, ah, might be a cousin. I'll have

107

to take that up with Mr. Dawson, I suppose. Thank you very much, you've been most helpful."

A pair of red-winged blackbirds made noisy, amorous love in the branches above his head as Lone Wolf Baylor went about setting up camp for the night. Far off, where the purple shadows already darkened the east, a solitary coyote warmed up for his nightly serenade. Clear on the peaceful air, the approach of three horses could be heard. Lone Wolf tensed slightly and laid a hand on his Model 73 Colt Peacemaker.

"Hello the camp," came a friendly hail.

"Howdy," Lone Wolf answered back. "You're in mighty empty parts. Ride in and show yourselves. Might be there's some coffee with your names on it."

"Knowed there was two of us, eh?" came the reply, with a chuckle. "Bet you made out the packhorse, too."

"Sure enough. C'mon in." Although he would have preferred to be alone, Lone Wolf decided that being cordial would attract less attention.

Cookpots and gold pans clanging, the pair rode into sight and halted again. A tall, lean man with dark hair and beard raised his hand in the universal peace sign. Lone Wolf studied them a moment, then motioned for them to advance.

"Mighty nice of you, Mister. T'name's Ramsey Carter," the bearded one declared.

"Cash Lewis," Lone Wolf responded, picking a convenient alias.

"This here's Newt Ames," Carter went on. "We're set on prospecting."

"Headed the wrong way, aren't you?" Lone Wolf inquired while the men dismounted and picketed their horses.

"Nope. Black Hills are gettin' too crowded. We figgered to head out Yellowstone way. Maybe try our luck far's Virginia City." Carter nodded toward Lone Wolf's new Model '76 Winchester. "Mighty nice lookin' iron you got there."

"They just got out this way. The Seventy-six model," Lone Wolf answered.

"Beats mine by a ways. Out here a man needs the best; a sixgun, rifle, maybe even a shotgun, and a knife or two. Wouldn't happen to have any spares, would you?"

"Why d'you ask?" Lone Wolf came back, instantly cautious.

"Thought I might make you an offer for that Seventy-six," Carter replied blandly.

"No way I'd consider that," Lone Wolf stated flatly. "It would take some talking to get a spare off me, if I had one, that is."

Carter and Ames came up with some fresh antelope to be added to the pot and settled back to sip coffee laced with whiskey while it cooked. Through the quiet hours of early evening they talked of growing activity in the Black Hills and the prospects for a man to get rich further out west. To Lone Wolf's continuing unease, the conversation kept returning to his destination and how he was armed.

"Too bad you ain't headed for the Yellowstone," Carter observed as he licked meat juices from his fingers. "Reckon as how you'd make a boon traveling companion."

"I'll take that as a compliment, Carter," Lone Wolf told him. "As it is, I've a mind to head a might bit further north."

"Oh? That's Crow country up there, ain't it?" Ames observed.

"Yep. And Cheyenne," Lone Wolf added. "The Crow have been given a reservation near where Custer got wiped out. There's a regular white community buildin' up near it. Name of Hardin. Thought I would look into possibilities there," Lone Wolf invented to account for his destination.

Ramsey Carter shook his head. "Don't know if I'd want that many Injuns around me. Well . . ." he said through a prodigious yawn. "Think I'll turn in."

"Me, too," Ames concurred. "Daylight comes too early in these parts."

With the fire well banked and hardly glowing, the camp settled down. Only light snores came from the slumbering men, with an occasional stamp or snort from a horse. Lone Wolf slept lightly, turned so he could instantly take in the entire encampment by simply opening his eyes. Shortly after midnight, when even the cicadas and crickets had given off their serenades, a slight sound pierced his dozing state.

Through slitted eyes, Lone Wolf saw shadowy movement from across the fire ring. He held his breath, keen ears interpreting each faint rustle, crunch and creak of leather. After the initial noise, silence held for nearly five minutes. Lone Wolf began to suspect he had been mistaken. Then a bootsole crunched on fine gravel behind him. While he swiftly rolled over, the Colt revolver in his hand made four distinctive clicks as he racked back the hammer.

Poised above him was Ramsey Carter, a short-handled axe raised in one hand. It took no great imagination for Lone Wolf to know he was the target for murder. He triggered the Colt at once, muzzle blast singeing his woolen blanket as the big 230 grain slug sped toward the target.

Ramsey Carter grunted and staggered back a step when the bullet smacked solidly into his stomach. He dropped the axe and clutched at his middle. At once a bright orange flash bloomed across the fire pit. Hot lead thumped into the ground only an inch from Lone Wolf's hip. His finger twitched on the trigger and a second round sped to strike Carter in the breast bone.

"Unngh!" Carter grunted. "I'll get you for that, Baylor," he panted out, revealing a knowledge he had kept concealed through the evening.

Lone Wolf shot him again. Ramsey Carter shuddered, took an uncertain step forward and fell on his face. Instantly, Lone Wolf directed his fire at the would-be back-shooter, Ames.

One more shot and the hammer fell on an empty chamber. Ames gave a brief yip of triumph. Bullets showered around Lone Wolf as he scrambled over the ground toward the fallen Carter. He recovered a Merwin and Hulbert .44 and snapped off a fast shot at Ames. A grunt of pain rewarded his efforts.

With the sound, Lone Wolf dove to the left, though not before an orange flower erupted into the night and a slug snapped past close to his head. He squeezed off another round and moved once more. Silence answered the pounding of his heart. Lone Wolf waited tensely. His breathing slowed and the thumping in his chest marked the time. When ten minutes went by without any sign or sound of his enemy, Lone Wolf cautiously raised in a crouch and covered the open space to the opposite side of the fire.

There he found no sign of Newton Ames. Tense, exercising extreme caution, Lone Wolf began a slow spiral around the camp. He'd made three-quarters of the first circuit when his Palouse gelding snorted indignantly, another horse grunted in protest of a sudden burden. Hoofs pounded a moment later and the wounded man raced away from the camp. Lone Wolf cursed silently. Rather than decrease his danger, it only served to make matters worse.

He could never safely go back to sleep. Nor could he build a fire and make coffee, Lone Wolf considered. To do either would only serve to make him vulnerable to the murder-minded Ames. Why had they done it? Lone Wolf pondered that puzzler while he waited out the hours to daylight. Suddenly Carter's last words echoed in his mind.

"I'll get you for that, *Baylor*."

They had known his real name and used it. Which meant they must be scouts for the gang that sought him. Why were they seeking him and how many did they actually number? With these uncomfortable thoughts to companion him, Lone Wolf sweated out the time before pink and white bands on the eastern horizon would free him from self-imposed confinement.

"Fire in the hole!" Joey's thin, piping voice rang up from inside the mine.

A moment later, he, Badger and *Pangeca* scrambled

112

out through the entrance. A dull whumph followed, then a thick billow of dust and acrid powder smoke. As the subterranean rumbles subsided, their boots crunched on the rubble-strewn ground as they made ready to return to the lateral head. Beaver entered first. Tyback had been imposed upon by his partner enough to provide boots, but not trousers.

Constant exposure to rock dust caused the boys to choose to work in the nude, rather than suffer more. Their skin, Joey decided, and tried to convince the other pair, was toughening to it. What bothered him more than their nakedness, Joey admitted only to himself, was that he occasionally caught Red Tyback eyeing them in an odd, inexplicable way. It made the hair on Joey's neck rise. Particularly the time Tyback wore that expression and placed his hand on *Pangeca*'s shoulder and let it slide to the small of his back.

"Awh kier!" Badger called out in imitation of the English words he had been taught as safety man for the blasts.

Joey and *Pangeca* led the way, with Mule-Ear and Red bringing up the rear, pushing a heavy minecar. Rock and gold ore would be loaded and removed, while the boys examined the ceiling for fissures that indicated where shoring would be needed. Tyback and Johnson had argued repeatedly over developing a system that would provide for enlarging the laterals and stopes so that the men could work below ground, hauling out larger quantities of ore than the boys could push. The one called Mule-Ear seemed to have a genuine concern for their welfare, Joey had noticed early on. As a result, he did his best to play up to the brown haired, bearded miner.

113

That hadn't so far resulted in their acquiring suitable work clothes or in getting more to eat. Joey staggered slightly as he canted down an angled stope, his belly aching for nourishment, though only ten-thirty in the morning. His muscles, like those of his friends, had hardened, yet they had lost weight. Joey's ribs stuck out and his heart-shaped face had become gaunt and ferret-like. Badger had lost his soft padding of baby fat and would soon look like a skeleton. Constantly in danger of being maimed or killed far underground, the boys had manifested their anxiety in nail-biting and various nervous tics. None of them had received the lash more than twice following their early attempt at escape, yet the threat remained constantly over them.

What worried Joey more even than these circumstances, he saw a daily decline in Badger and *Pangeca*. The Oglala boys had confided that they would willingly lie down and die, rather than live such a miserable life. Joey recognized a similar attitude within himself. No matter how hungry he got, he sometimes didn't care if he ate or not. Joey pushed away such reflections and hefted his pick-axe to pry at the thin vein of gold-bearing ore in the flickering light of his carbide lamp. Tonight, he thought, they would talk about escape again.

Chapter 11

"I say you're full of shit!" Peter Dillon barked at Sheldon Boyle.

"You want to put some money on it?" Boyle challenged. "I know I can draw and fire a shot 'fore you can clap your hands together."

"You only *think* you're fast," Peter taunted. "Do you think you could do it 'fore I could draw and fire?"

"Hah! That's easy. You're slow as an old woman."

"Knock off that horsecrap and get over here," Loomis Clutter called in a bored tone. "We've got things to talk about."

Camped in the western slopes of the Black Hills, the gang had awaited news about Lone Wolf Baylor's movements since his cold, merciless killing of three men a week earlier.

An hour past, the wounded scout had ridden in to make his report. After the first few words, Clutter and Tulley had taken the rest in private. They had now apparently reached some conclusion. Bored, the ne'er-do-wells and frontier riff-raff of the *Venganza* gang gathered around. Gloved fists on his hips, Loomis Clutter looked at the sullen faces. When the silence

115

grew tense, he nodded to Lane Tulley.

"Lane, you tell them."

"Baylor killed Ramsey Carter and wounded Newt. He's definitely headed to Crow country. Which makes for a good reason *not* to pursue him in my book. I say we put out feelers to locate Rebecca Caldwell. When she gets hers, it'll bring Baylor a-runnin'. Once we got him mad and careless, our job will be easy. What do the rest of you think?"

"I'm for doing like we said," Niel Mallory offered. "First we go for Baylor, then the girl."

"Loomis agrees with you," Tulley informed him. "Who else has somethin' to say?"

"There any little girls around where she is?" Paddy O'Toole asked.

"Shut up, you son of a bitch," Al Honeycutt growled.

"Paddy's right," Ike MacKinnon spoke up. "I'm gettin' as horny as a three-peckered bull. When we catch up to this Caldwell gal, we don't have to kill her right off, do we? Maybe have a little fun first?"

Several voices chorused agreement. Lane Tulley raised a hand for silence. "She's deadlier than Baylor," he reminded them. "I think I'd want her tied up real tight before I tried anything."

Peter Dillon stepped ahead of the semi-circle of hardcases. "I'm getting tired of building saddle sores and never catching those two. Gettin' tired of lopin' my mule, for that matter," he added with a blush. "We ought to do something positive or give up on the whole thing."

"You anxious to get back to Ill-i-nois and rape some more little girls, Petey?" Sheldon Boyle sneered.

116

Peter flushed a dark crimson. Before anyone could react, Peter filled his hand with the solid buttstock of his .32-20 Colt. "You bastard!" he yelled.

Al Honeycutt, standing closest, whipped his hand out and dropped his right thumb into the space between the hammer and frame of Peter's sixgun. His fingers curled around the cylinder and trigger guard. Peter threw him a startled glance and Al shook his head in a negative gesture.

"Well, that settles one thing," Matt Wellington breathed out softly. "Peter is one hell of a lot faster than Boyle. Now, why don't you put it up, Peter? We've no call to fight amongst ourselves."

"He's got no call to bad-mouth me like that if he doesn't want to back it up," Peter said hotly.

A thoroughly chastened, and still frightened, Sheldon Boyle took a hesitant step forward and put out his hand in a sign of reconciliation. "I'm sorry, Pete. Really I am. It's just . . . sometimes I forget. You are sort of small, an' young lookin'. I guess I figure you had still ought to be out behind the barn whackin' off, instead of ridin' with an outfit like this. If you'll take my hand, I'll not prod you again."

Peter holstered his revolver and wet dry lips. "A-all right, Shell. Here, let's shake. But remember, I'm seventeen. I've been on my own for five years. I quit whackin' off behind the barn, or in the haymow for that matter, before I ran away from home."

"Kinda touchy about that, eh?" Sheldon prodded. Then he raised both hands before him, palms out, fingers splayed, in a sign of surrender. "No, no. Only teasin', no offense meant."

Clutter cleared his throat loudly. "About the matter

117

of Baylor," he began, drawing tension from the situation. "We seem to be of mixed opinion. What about a compromise? Those who want to go after Baylor, no matter the cost, do so. The rest can stay here, develop information on Rebecca Caldwell and wait for news from the others."

"What say we hit another bank while we're waitin'?" Al Honeycutt suggested. "I'm kinda gettin' low on money."

"I'll go for that," Lane Tulley added.

"Don't. Oh, please don't," Tommy Archer sobbed pitifully in English.

He cradled the head and shoulders of Moon Son in his lap. The slightly built Sioux boy had received a savage beating with fists and boots earlier in the day. To make it worse, the error, which had caused a cave-in, had been *Mahtolasan*'s fault. Moon Son had taken the blame and suffered terribly for it. On top of that this was a Saturday and Hiram Coulter, who had bought them, would be away to Deadwood City until late Sunday. The boys would be chained, but able to move about camp and prepare all the food they wanted for the better part of two glorious days. Then had come the beating, with curses and threats. For an hour or so, Moon Son had lain supine, his breathing shallow, complexion overcast with a sickly gray. Then he had cried out weakly.

"Grandfather, Grandfather, I'm coming." He sighed and lay still.

Coulter had been gone for three hours. Darkness filled the camp, yet Tommy didn't move. In his anguish over the death of his friend, he had lost command of the Lakota tongue. Moon Son had grown cold and stiff in Tommy's arms. Great salt tears ran down the tow-headed lad's face and he felt an unutterable misery. What could he do now? Tormented, Tommy rocked back and forth, crooning to the dead boy in his lap.

Escape!

Emblazoned in tall letters of fire, Tommy saw the concept born in his head. First he would build a burial scaffold for Moon Son, then get away, locate *Pinspinzala* and they would strike out for home. Stiff from his hours of sitting in one position, Tommy worked his way out from under the corpse of his friend and shuffled out through the camp. He located a cold chisel and hammer and a small anvil. A few swift strokes broke the rivet that fixed the hinge on his waist collar. Free. Really free, he rejoiced. The image of his friend, so still, so cold, mouth and eyes slackly open, sobered Tommy.

Where would he build the scaffold? What would he use? Mind fighting off the numbness of grief, he went to a small stand of lodgepole pine, and began his task. He worked on until tormenting pangs of hunger reminded him he hadn't eaten since early Saturday morning. Dawn put pale bands of white, pink and orange along the horizon by the time Tommy had kindled a fire, prepared food and eaten it. With daylight, his task grew easier.

A well-sharpened axe bit through tender pine saplings. Tommy cut away the foliage, careful to leave four tall ones with "Y" notches to hold the framework he would construct next. He sweat as he dug holes

119

and set the corner posts. Tears blurred his eyes while he tied together the framework. His lean, hard body ached enough so he took time out to refresh himself in the creek before continuing. Shortly before noon, he had Moon Son wrapped in a blanket, with branches of sweet sage and laurel, his scant few possessions confined within the bundle. Now came the hard part.

Try as he might, Tommy could not lift the body alone. At last he thought of the block and tackle Coulter used around the mine. With this, he soon had the situation in control. Despite his determination to the contrary, Tommy wept for a solid fifteen minutes once he had placed the corpse in position.

"What to do now?" he asked himself aloud in a croaking voice, while he used a bony forearm to wipe his tears.

"Clean up!" Tommy answered himself. "A good long swim, then something to eat. Pack away some food." Put on his loincloth for the first time in a month, his mind filled in as he started for the water. "Then get away from here. Find Joey. He'll know how to take us home."

Spirits rising, Tommy entered into his tasks eagerly.

Two days later, his food running short, Tommy remained free. He had eluded all searches. Unfortunately, he had as yet to locate Joey Ridgeway. On that terrible day when they sold him to Coulter, Joey had been taken off to the north. Tommy went that direction, all the way to Alder Gulch. He had circled and crouched peering at various mine operations, only to find no sign of Joey. Joey had to be there somewhere, and somehow Tommy would find him.

He knew he would, because he had to.

Like every Monday morning, the Merchants' Bank of Farmingdale, Nebraska did a brisk business. Three clerks handled the steady flow of deposits, while two more handled other transactions. A dozen customers filled the lobby space when five men, wearing paisley scarf masks pushed their way inside.

"Everyone stand fast!" a tall, thin young man demanded.

"Holdup!" one teller gasped.

"I'm surprised you noticed," Lane Tulley said sarcastically. "Like I said, folks, stand still and no one gets hurt. Empty them drawers, boys. And don't forget the vault."

So far it had gone about average for bank robberies. Bills rustled like old leaves as handsful left cash drawers to be deposited in canvas bags. Stacks of five, ten, twenty and fifty dollar gold pieces rang musically. Then Lane Tulley noticed a new sound. An angry murmur came from the bank's patrons, growing in volume as he took note.

"Vile brigands," a buxom matron, her hair done in a bun, spat.

"I'll thank you to keep quiet, ma'am," Lane drawled.

"Low-life border trash," a man muttered darkly.

"Mister, you'd be smart not to push u—"

"We outnumber them, folks. What do you say?" another man shouted as he produced a short-barreled Colt revolver from under his coat.

Three sixguns spoke simultaneously, and a bullet tore through Cass Owen's chest, high on the right. He turned partway toward the door and his mask slipped from his nose, revealing his face. Lane Tulley made a try for the apparent leader of this resistance, only to find himself ducking slugs.

"Let's go, Lane," Niel Mallory urged from his place by the tellers' cages.

Tulley saw ample reason in that. "It's gettin' too hot, boys, let's pull out," he commanded.

Niel Mallory and Steve Horner reached the doorway at the same time a shotgun boomed from behind the high counter. Horner took most of the load of 00 buckshot in his side and head, spraying the walls and Mallory with blood.

"Yeow," Niel Mallory shouted as three heavy pellets ripped into the meaty portion of his upper back. He stumbled out the door.

Raymond Dawson and Peter Dillon followed. A moment later, Lane Tulley darted out onto the boardwalk. Almost at once, gunfire erupted from across the street.

Tommy Archer saw a flash of snow-white hair above the scrub brush near noon of Tuesday. His heart began to thump as he used all his remembered Indian skills to quietly slip closer. At thirty yards distance he heard scraps of conversation in Lakota. His heart pounded wildly. It had to be Joey. He tried a wounded rabbit cry to no avail. Then he did a fair imitation of a horned owl.

"Who's there?" came a shaky question in Lakota.

"Is that *Pinspinzala?*" Tommy asked cautiously.

"*Mahtolasan!*" a piping voice cried. "Is it really you?"

Quickly as that, Tommy Archer again became White Bear Cub. Caution forgotten, he rushed into the clearing at the Tyback-Johnson mine. In a wild show of emotion, he and Joey embraced, hugging each other and shedding a few tears of relief and joy. Then *Mahtolasan* exchanged equally enthusiastic greetings with *Hoka* and *Pangeca.*

"How . . . how did you get here?" *Pinspinzala* asked in wonder.

"I escaped on Saturday. M-my friend, Moon Son died of a beating. I felt so awful, then I decided to run away. First I buried Moon Son on a scaffold and then started looking for you." Tommy seemed to notice their chains for the first time. "If the men who bought you aren't here, why are you still chained?"

Joey and the others gave him a blank look. "Why *are we?*" Joey demanded of himself. "Help us, *Mahtolasan.* We'll get free and all run away."

Tyback had provided better quality chains, they soon discovered. After nearly an hour, *Pinspinzala* and only one of his companions had been freed. It even required an application of hammer and chisel to release the agile *Pangeca.* Quickly the boys set about preparing supplies for the journey to the east. They'd nearly finished when Mule-Ear Johnson and Jess Coulter stormed into camp.

"By God, you little devils, we'll fix you!" Coulter roared. "There! There's mine. Run away from my digs, will you? You little whelp, you put 'em up to this, didn't you?"

Scurrying and dodging, the boys attempted to evade the evil whites, so intent on reenslaving them. Joey threw a large rock at Coulter and cut to his left,

123

only to be wrapped in the strong arms of Mule-Ear.

"I got this one," the miner called out.

"I have one, too. Let's hog-tie 'em and get the rest," Coulter announced.

Within three minutes, *Hoka* and *Pangeca* had also been apprehended. "Now what?" Mule-Ear Johnson asked.

"I say beat 'em within an inch of their lives," Coulter advised.

"And wind up with what you got back at your digs?" Johnson accused.

"Say, now . . . are you sayin' my treatment of that Injun brat caused him to die?"

"These kids kin lie down and will themselves to death, if they want to. I've seen it done. Especially if they've gone through that dream stuff and the torture it takes to make one a man by their lights. Might be you ask that tow-headed one. I figger he speaks good English, like ours does," Johnson informed him.

"Him? Far's I could see, he was dumbest of the pair," Coulter responded.

"Let me. You, boy, what's your white name?" Mule-Ear asked gently.

"Go ahead an' tell him," Joey advised in Lakota.

"Tommy. Tommy Archer," *Mahtolasan* answered in a sullen tone.

"I'll be gol-danged. Well, come on, Tommy Archer, you 'n me are gettin' back to my claim."

"Hold on a minute, Jess. What say I take him off your hands. He'll be nothin' but trouble from now on, with only you to watch out for him."

"I put a lot of money into that brat," Coulter complained.

"You can get more from Hardesty. No more than a hundred apiece, I'd say. I'll give you one-fifty for this one and we can keep all the runners in one place."

Coulter pondered it a moment. "Done. And good riddance, too." He held out his hand for the payment.

Mule-Ear Johnson paid it out in nuggets. Then, while Coulter made his solitary departure, he turned to Tommy. "Well, boy, it looks like you've got yourself a new home."

Chapter 12

Bullets slapped the wooden fronts of buildings in Farmingdale as the *Venganza* gang ran for their horses. First to fall was the horse-holder, and four mounts ran wildly down the street, driven by the gunfire. So far, none of the outlaws had seen any sign of a man with a badge.

"Who the hell is that?" Matthew Wellington shouted over the tumult.

"Damned if I know," Lane Tulley responded. "You seen the law?"

"Nope. We'd better get out of the open, go after the horses," Matt suggested.

"Don't I just know it," Lane agreed. He looked around to find three of the gang mounted. "Go after our mounts. Meet us one street over."

Using the horses for cover, Lane, Matt and Peter ran for an alleyway.

"How'd this come about?" Peter asked nervously.

"Wish I knew," Lane answered as he thumbed off two rounds toward the unknown enemy barricaded across the street.

Earlier in the morning, Rebecca and Whirlwind
had ridden into town, following the three men identi-
fied as being with those seeking Lone Wolf. They also
planned to obtain supplies before moving on. When
the trio they followed were met by five more, their
interest increased. When the five newcomers pulled
masks over their faces and entered the bank, Rebecca
and her companion remained puzzled, but had little
doubt as to what might be afoot.

"No time to locate the local law," Rebecca remarked.
"Find good cover on this side of the street. When they
come out, we'll open up. That should draw the
marshal soon enough."

Whirlwind frowned. "If Big Ears hears shooting, he
might come to our aid."

A grim smile lifted the corners of Rebecca's mouth
and she pushed back her raven hair. "Wouldn't that be
too bad for our friends over there?"

She and Whirlwind had hardly located firing posi-
tions when shots came from inside the bank. Something had gone wrong. A moment later, the outlaws
began to emerge. Rebecca rose from behind a filled
water trough.

"Now, let them have it!" she called.

Lead cracked through the air. Rebecca aimed her
Smith American for the horse holder and brought him
down with two fast shots. Whirlwind crouched behind
some barrels of merchandise in from the the general
mercantile. He wounded one of the gunmen and took
aim at another when the horses panicked and ran off

127

down the street. At once the holdup men used them for cover as they sprinted to an alleyway.

"They're getting away," Whirlwind complained.

"We'll go after them. Can't get far on foot," Rebecca declared.

They recovered their own horses and galloped to the corner, rounded it and pounded down on the startled hardcases. Feeling trapped, the outlaws put up a determined resistance. Bullets cracked past Rebecca's head. She felt a slight tug when one bit through the flying skirt of her elkhide dress. Faced by such superior firepower, she signaled for them to turn away. Off to one side she saw three men returning with the strayed horses.

Quickly, the gang members mounted. They'd be after her and Whirlwind in a second, Rebecca realized. Would they be able to outrun her swift Palouse, *Síla?* She'd soon find out, a rumble of hoofs told her. In the midst of the whirling, dusty confusion, more shots sounded.

Men yelled and raced across a small lawn, directing their wild-eyed mounts between houses in an attempt to escape an unseen danger. They fired wildly into buildings as they passed. The cause of their panic became clear to Rebecca when Big Ears and the Indian Police of the Badger Society rumbled through the street and streaked after the fleeing robbers.

When the gang split into twos and singles, and sped away in different directions, the Oglala horsemen gave up pursuit. Quietly, in a rough column of threes they rode back into Farmingdale. By then the town law had joined Rebecca and Whirlwind. He gaped at the approaching riders.

"Well, I never. To think that our old enemy, the Sioux, would ever come to the aid of the town."

"Two men throw away these," Big Ears said proudly, through a triumphant grin, as he hefted heavily laden canvas bags.

"Ya . . . ya saved the bank's money," the bug-eyed marshal spluttered.

More townspeople filled the street, gaping at the Indians and chattering like a barnyard full of hens. Rebecca looked around, taking stock.

"Marshal, you have three men down, wounded, but able to answer questions. There are several things we'd like to learn also. Would you mind if we conducted the questioning?"

"Would your Sioux friends be in on it?" the lawmen asked warily. Rebecca gave him an impish grin. "Well then, I think we might be surprised by how much they could tell us."

"Keep them away! Keep them away from me," Finn Brockman screamed as Big Ears and another Oglala warrior approached him some fifteen minutes later.

"You tell us what you're doing and why, and we might consider that," Rebecca told him coldly.

"Marshal, you wouldn't let these heathens torture me," Finn wailed in supplication.

Marshal Vickors produced a grim expression. He'd only moments before received a report of injured townspeople. "Mrs. Pritchard, she was the mother of seven children under twelve. One of you bastards put a bullet through her kitchen window *and through her head!*" he ended in a shout.

"And you ask me if I'd let these Sioux at you. Mister, Mrs. Pritchard was a widow and a friend of mine. Now there's seven little waifs without a momma, that the town will have to care for. I don't give a rip if they cut off your balls and feed 'em to you. Pardon, ma'am," he added for Rebecca's sake.

"No offense, Marshal Vickors. I was going to suggest the same thing. First, though, I thought we might start with cutting off finger joints."

The grizzled lawman produced a reasonable expression of horror. "You mean . . . one . . . at . . . a time?"

"Exactly. Snip—snip—snip. Start with his trigger finger. Then the index finger of the other hand. Then come back and get his middle finger . . . and so on."

"Stop—stop—*stop!*" Brockman wailed in terror.

"Why are you robbing banks in this area?" Rebecca asked sweetly.

"For what else? To get money," Brockman's surly reply came flatly.

"Why do you need that much money? Why ride with a gang?" Rebecca doubled on him.

"Takes money to run a big operation. That's what Loomis said. Besides, we got a good reason to be together."

"Whatever might that be?" Rebecca inquired lightly.

"Got nothin' to do with a bank holdup," Finn Brockman stated defiantly.

"We'll leave that for a while. Tell me instead the reason you're following Lone Wolf Baylor?"

With a frightfully cold emptiness expanding inside, Finn Brockman suddenly realized who this woman, dressed like a Sioux squaw, had to be. His chin began to tremble and his eyes darted from side to side, taking in the room of grim, determined faces. His heart started to palpitate, skipping a beat, and the sphincter muscle controlling his bladder released. In his fear and humiliation, Finn realized his bowels would not be far behind. Despite his fright, he remained defiant.

"Go to hell. I ain't tellin' you nothin'."

Rebecca said something curt and guttural in Lakota. Whirlwind and Big Ears moved forward. Rebecca spoke again, in English, for Brockman's benefit. "We're not going to do it the easy way with a pair of wire nippers," she explained. "Use the tomahawk, *Tatekohom'ni.*"

For the first time, Finn Brockman saw that one held a wooden block, the other a tomahawk. He began to writhe against his bonds, and an animal howl came from his distorted lips. Big Ears placed the block in position on the table, under Finn's hand. Roughly he spread the fingers, isolating the first next to the thumb.

"Take the whole finger, to prove we're not bluffing," Rebecca rapped harshly.

Brockman's howl became a banshee wail of the tormented damned. Eyes squinted tightly shut, head turned away in a reflexive attempt to avoid the danger, Finn Brockman felt a momentary touch of cold and a strong blow.

"Good, clean cut," he heard Rebecca's voice remark clinically.

Instantly, Finn Brockman fainted. Immediately Whirlwind tossed away the sliver of ice he had concealed in his hand. Rebecca set to work with strips of white cloth and a small jar of chicken blood. When all was in readiness, a bucket of cold water in the face revived Brockman. His hand had been heavily bandaged, a large red spot showing where his finger had been.

"Left hand next," he heard the dreaded command.

"No, *No!* Please, please not again. I'll tell you everything." Quickly Brockman outlined the manner in which they had all been contacted, their relationships to the old Tulley gang and the identities of all he could recall, in particular, Lane Tulley, Loomis Clutter and Paddy O'Toole. He even revealed how they had determined that Lone Wolf had headed for the Crow reservation and how many followed him. At the end, gasping with fear and exertion, he concluded with a plea.

"That's all. I've told you everything I know. I — I'm crippled now. You — you'll let me go, won't you?" His eyes grew large in eloquent supplication.

Slowly, Rebecca shook her head. "There's a matter of several killings related to that bank job. I'd like to do some real harm to you myself, but I think justice will be served well enough if we leave you here so Marshal Vickors can hang you."

"I'll do anything — anything. Please don't . . ." The meaning behind Rebecca's earlier words reached him. "What do you mean do me real harm? Haven't you done enough?"

"Release his left arm, Whirlwind," Rebecca commanded. "Unwrap those bandages, Brockman. I think you'll find nothing's been done to you at all, except in your imagination."

Birds twittered in the branches above. Lone Wolf

paused by the narrow, icy creek and drank deeply of the water. It tasted of crawfish, algae and tadpoles. While he rested in the shade, he let his senses expand. Instinct had always been a large part of the hunting and warfare skills of the plains tribes. His search into the esoteric regions of Crow religion had heightened his perceptions enormously over the average person. His ears and eyes seemed to travel back over the trail he had pursued. While they did, his mind sorted through all he observed. Each bent slip of grass, a turned stone, animal droppings. All told a story of solitude, and thus, safety. Yet some persistent nagging sensation told him the present serenity was but an illusion. In an effort to shake it off, he bent and took another drink.

"I'll get to seeing things next," he said aloud to his horse. "What do you think of that, Thunderer?"

The powerful gelding snorted, shivered his loose coat, and stamped a front hoof. Another wet and noisy rumble came through his nostrils and Thunderer turned his long graceful neck, to look off in the direction from which they had come. Instantly, Lone Wolf rose to his feet. He stepped into the stream, the reins in one hand, and led his mount along. With as rapid a pace as he could make, Lone Wolf led Thunderer along for better than two miles. Then they emerged, on the opposite side of the creek, and rode due north for a quarter mile, until a low, rolling ridge separated the natural passage from another, broader valley.

Lone Wolf marked it well, remembering that it was here, on that finger ridge now to the south of him, that Capt. William Fetterman and the survivors of his

133

command met their end on December 21, 1866. Ironically, earlier that fall, Fetterman had bragged that given eighty men he would ride through the entire Sioux Nation. When provided with exactly that number to effect a rescue of the wood train, under attack by the Sioux, Red Cloud of the Sioux, and Roman Nose of the Cheyenne delighted in proving him wrong. It would serve its purpose today, he decided, in his own impending battle.

"He took to the water here, th' tricky devil," Loomis Clutter announced after studying the sign around the creek. "We'll follow until we find out where he left the crick, then make camp for the night."

An hour later, those men who went upstream located the spot. A messenger was dispatched to bring back the others and a comfortable camp laid out amid the rocks and stunted blackjack pine. Willows and clear cold water provided extra luxury. Four men went out to make meat, bottles appeared and the idlers set out to gather firewood. When sunset purpled the sky, the men had been fed and bottles once more made the rounds. By ten o'clock, only soft snores and the dying glow of well-banked coals marked their presence.

It took little effort for Lone Wolf to locate the encampment in the dark. On moccasined feet, he slipped in close and paused, listening intently. The rasping breath of several of the hunters positioned them for him. A soft grunt and the flare of a match pointed out a guard by the picketed horses. Off toward the narrow stream a man cleared his throat. Lone Wolf let an estimated fifteen minutes pass, then made his move.

Cold steel bit into vulnerable flesh. The sentry seated beside the picket line drummed his feet on the yielding ground in a soft tattoo of death, while Lone Wolf held a hand over his mouth. Blade still wet from the throat cutting, Lone Wolf applied it to the crown of the dead man's head. The scalp-lock made a zipper-like tearing sound when he pulled it away. Stealthily, Lone Wolf headed for the only other nightwatch.

Again the knife flashed in starlight and slid deeply into corded muscle and the tough cartilage of a human larynx. Bloody froth bubbled from the turned-back lips of the wound. Once more, Lone Wolf scalped his victim, before ghosting off toward the picket line. There he cut each end of the main rope, and drifted away into the night.

Moments later, a wavering flutter of burning pine needles, attached to the tip of an arrow, sped into the camp. Where it struck mattered little to Lone Wolf, only that it continue to burn. Quickly he launched another, a third following closely behind. By the time the fourth, and last, arced into the night sky, Lone Wolf had started off to where he left his horse and gear. In the camp, sudden, rude awakenings filled the air with curses and shouts of alarm.

"Fire!" Ike MacKinnon shouted, rousing from deep slumber at the odor of burning pine pitch. "B'God, it's firearrows!"

"Over here, there's another," Loomis Clutter shouted.

Lone Wolf's third fiery messenger landed by the severed picket line. Brush flared and the horses took instant fright, their sensitive nostrils recording smoke and heat. With shrill squeals and nervous whinnies, they edged away, testing the lines that held them. When they encountered no resistance, they wheeled and thrashed about, lining along the creek bank as they raced away from the threat their dim brains perceived.

"It's Baylor!" Clutter bellowed. "Goddamn him!" he yelled as the horses began to gallop blindly away from camp. "Baylor, you *baaaastard!*" he screamed as he saw the fourth arrow, which had landed among the pack-saddles, and helplessly watched their supplies begin to burn.

Chapter 13

Armed now with a direction to follow, Rebecca, Whirlwind and the Badger Police set out after the remaining avengers. For once, the weather favored them. A china-blue sky, dotted with puffy balls of white, a tiny point of brazen sun washing the top of the azure dome to translucent alabaster raised the spirits of them all. The air smelled of growing things, even in the vast stretches of sage-covered sandy hills. Their light-hearted attitude continued until Rebecca spotted a tall, black column of smoke on the horizon.

"Trouble for someone," she observed to Whirlwind.

Big Ears produced a big smile. "I would say Dakota raiders. But we aren't raiding any more."

"Now that you're an Indian Policeman, your outlook has surely changed, Big Ears," Rebecca observed.

Through a chuckle, Big Ears contradicted her. "No it hasn't. Not even the enemy has changed. There are bad whites, there are bad red men. Now I can punish both."

His response brought general laughter. The miles slowly closed between them and the column of smoke. It rose straight and challenging in the still air, giving off streamers of white on occasion, then darkening with ominous import. At two miles distance, with a low swell intervening, they could see sparks rising. Atop the ridge, they gazed down into a low valley.

There lay the ruins of what had once been a prosperous ranching operation. The main house, and two smaller ones, a bunkhouse, two large barns, and several trees showed blackened skeletons to the cheerful sky. In the ranch yard, several huddled bundles spoke of violent death. Riding closer, Rebecca began to scowl darkly.

"Did you see them?" she asked, referring to the distinctive hoof marks they had been following for two days.

"Yes. This was not done by Indians," Whirlwind declared. "The men we follow came here. Why did they kill their own kind? People who would not have harmed them?"

"Man's been trying to answer those questions since the beginning of time, Whirlwind," Rebecca responded philosophically. Then, more to the point, "They're animals. Men gone wild. Oh, God, women and children, too," she choked out as they neared the scene of slaughter. "They've gone beyond even their own self-restraints now. We've *got* to stop them, Whirlwind."

Lookout Point formed one of a pair of sharp, cone-shaped peaks that marked the natural pass through rising ground toward the northwest. Beyond lay the ruins of Fort Phil Kearny, burned by Red Cloud and the Sioux after the Army wisely withdrew. Rebecca and her followers rode a portion of the Bozeman Trail now, eyes sharp for any sign of the men they sought. Down in the narrow meander of valley, where the trail led toward the site of Fetterman's downfall, they came upon the stream.

"Good time to freshen the horses," Rebecca suggested. She pointed ahead to a cluster of willows and blackjack pine. "We can stop there, let them drink and eat a little and have a meal ourselves."

Whirlwind nodded agreement. When they entered the grove of trees, the first sight of importance they encountered was a pair of fresh earth mounds. A quick reading of the signs told the story.

"Lone Wolf," Rebecca stated positively. "He knows he is being followed by men who want to kill him. It looks like he's making it difficult for them."

"What they don't know is that we're right behind," Whirlwind added. "When we catch them between us, we'll smash them easily."

"They'll concentrate on Lone Wolf. We," Rebecca planned aloud, "will hit them in the rear. The men with Loomis Clutter cannot survive that."

Two hours later they reached the small settlement of Sheridan. The first news to assail them came from a dozen people standing around Ketcham's General Mercantile. Clearly, from the midst of the crowd, came the word, "Robbed."

"Yeah," Sam Ketcham, the proprietor, spoke up. "Cleaned out all the cash, took twenty boxes of ammunition and two sides of bacon. Killed Mister Beesley, too. For no reason."

No further explanation was needed for Rebecca. Grim-faced, she rode on, her small entourage in double file behind.

Will Hardesty, thumbs hooked into the front waist-band of his trousers, stood between the doorway and Lotta Crabtree's desk in the Deadwood City bordello. He had his hat set at a rakish angle and with his head canted quizzically to one side, the cocky expression he wore irritated more than his words.

"How do you mean the price is going up?" Lotta grated through clenched teeth. Her faded ginger hair, done in sausage curls shook with anger.

Her small, mean mouth puckered wetly and her avaricious green eyes sparkled with the lust to get the better of any bargain.

"Just what I'm tellin' you, Lotta. It's gettin' harder and harder to round up any Injun kids. Their folks are keepin' them closer to home and the agencies are patrolled night and day. When our risks go up, the price goes up. One-fifty each for this lot."

"Where's your mask and gun, Will? That's plain robbery. Hell, man, those Sioux girls ain't all that much, you ask me. Most of 'em have to be taught right from the git-go. The one good thing I can say about 'em is that they don't seem to mind bein' naked, or to have a naked man around them. Only time I make any real money on one of them is when some miner has a son or a nephew who's turned thirteen or fourteen and the old man wants to get the kid's cherry popped. Those little boys don't seem so shy, or con-fused, if the girl's one around their own age.

"Other than that, them redskins don't hardly earn their keep. 'Sides, there's been more than should up

140

and die on me. The last one right underneath her first trick. Scared the old buzzard witless. *And* he demanded his money back."

"I'm sorry for your inconvenience, Lotta. In truth I am. But the merchandise is sold 'as is' and let the buyer beware. Sorry, but no refunds."

"I ain't asking for my money back. Only for better goods," Lotta snapped.

"Well, there I can promise you some good news. I'll be able to provide older, stronger girls before long. Won't necessarily be Injuns, either. There's a whole colony of Swedes or Dutchies over near the Minnesota border. We figgered to drop by and see what the goods are like."

"Now there you go," Lotta enthused. "I think they are just what these miners like. It's only a few of 'em hunger after the li'l Injun girls. You bring me some Swede girls, or Germans, I'll be glad to pay higher. Now then, won't you consider one and a quarter for these you brought tonight?"

By pushing hard, Rebecca and her Indian Police caught up lost time. In the wide valley of the Tongue River, they cut fresh sign of the outlaws, also the peculiar pattern of Lone Wolf's Palouse, Thunderer.

"Less than an hour ahead," Rebecca estimated. "We can catch them before nightfall."

"What do we do then?" Whirlwind inquired.

"You and I will circle around and try to locate Lone Wolf. While we do, Big Ears and the Badgers will get in position to attack the gang. When everything is ready, or in case they attack Lone Wolf, Big Ears will

141

hit them in the rear."

Half an hour later, wisps of dust in the air and small dots, moving in the distance, revealed the gang's location. Immediately, Rebecca and Whirlwind split off from the others, climbing the sloping bluff to the north, onto a rolling plain that stretched far in the desired direction. They rode at a fast canter, not the least worried about the outlaws discovering their presence.

"It shouldn't be far," Rebecca theorized as they forded Goose Creek a quarter mile above its mouth. "I can . . . almost *feel* Lone Wolf's presence."

"That is to be understood. You have been close for a long time," Whirlwind told her.

"We'll split up here, circle north and I'll take the south, down through the Tongue Valley. One of us is bound to find his camp. If whoever doesn't find Lone Wolf continues to circle we'll get together eventually. Then we can lay some plans."

Sage and columbine, lupine and daisies sent sweet messages heavenward as Rebecca rode through the rampant prairie brush, bruising leaves and flowers. Quail and meadowlarks, field mice and other small creatures scattered at her approach. Twenty minutes went by and Rebecca's sensitive nose detected the odor of a sweaty horse and pine bark tinder. Someone was building a fire not far ahead. Quietly she dismounted and walked *Sila* toward the scents. She stepped into a low clearing, under the wide branches of a cottonwood before she realized it was there.

A low fire burned in a small ring of rocks. A large parfleche bag hung from a stub of an old broken-off branch. Otherwise the campsite lay empty.

142

"A person could get shot that way, Becky," Lone Wolf said from behind her.

Rebecca turned to face him. "You're a hard man to catch, Lone Wolf."

"I try to be," he answered dryly. "Those men back there seem to have other ideas. Figure to get me before I reach the Crow agency."

"They'll not do that," Rebecca replied confidently. "I have twenty-seven Oglala police with me. They're trailing the men hunting you. Do you . . . do you know why they're after you?"

"No, I can't say I do. Any ideas?"

"We caught three of them in the midst of a bank robbery. They're all relatives of members of Jake Tulley's gang. They're out to get revenge on you and me. Now we have a chance to turn the tables on them."

Lone Wolf produced a grin. "In more ways than one," he informed her. "I have a little surprise of my own to spring on them. In the meanwhile, it's good to see you again. It's been a long winter." Lone Wolf produced a meaningful expression.

"The hurt is still there. Grover is gone and nothing can bring him back. Peter—Peter's dead, too and I ache everytime I see in my mind his sweet smile and freckled nose, the way he'd stand, hip-shot, and watch me in the kitchen for hours. Ah, loving . . . why does it have to be so painful when it ends?"

"Be grateful it does," Lone Wolf counseled. "So many times love turns into something bitter and ugly. You were happy with your man and your children. Uh, Joey's all right, isn't he?"

"N-no," Rebecca choked, aware again of their primary mission. "Or rather, I don't know. He—he's been stolen from the agency. We don't know by whom, or where he went, but the best bet is a mine somewhere in the Black Hills."

"A mine? As a slave laborer? By the Great Lance! You know I'll help you find him," Lone Wolf offered sincerely.

"Thank you, I had hoped you would. With you, we're thirty strong. I have some leads, but the main thing is to get all of the missing children back. More than thirty have been taken from the reservations so far," Rebecca revealed.

"Any chance that we can do so?" Lone Wolf asked, always practical.

"I think so," Rebecca told him in a small voice.

"Always the optimist." Lone Wolf paused and made a sign for silence. "Someone out there."

"Too soon for the outlaws chasing you. It must be Whirlwind."

Lone Wolf produced a smile. "You mean the young warrior you showed so much favor up at the Greasy Grass four years ago?"

"The same," Rebecca agreed.

"Can you call him in?" Lone Wolf inquired.

"I think so." Rebecca puckered her lips and whistled a fair bluejay call.

Five seconds passed and a crested woodpecker answered. She called again. Brush crackled and limbs parted to reveal Whirlwind and his horse. Once the amenities had been observed, they discussed the problem. Each had a differing idea, and Lone Wolf still did not reveal his "surprise." At the conclusion, they settled on a plan.

"You will take news of what we will do to the *Ihokapi*," Rebecca instructed Whirlwind. "Then return here. In the morning, Lone Wolf will take up a position which will expose him to the gang when they get started from their camp. When they follow, we attack the leaders from the sides. Then Lone Wolf springs his surprise. Shortly after that, the Badger Society hits them in the rear."

"It should be a massacre," Whirlwind enthused.

Rebecca winced. "Don't use that word. If we're decided, how about something to eat? I'm starving."

Chapter 14

Woodsmoke and the scent of brewing coffee. God, how he loved it. Loomis Clutter threw aside the blanket which had covered him through the night and stood, easing his stiff joints. A yawn and stretch and he found himself ready for a steaming cup of coffee, after putting on his boots. Stomping them into place, he crossed to the fire.

" 'Morning, Mister Clutter," Peter Dillon greeted.

"You up first, Peter?"

"I had last watch, remember, Mr. Clutter?" Peter responded.

"Oh, that's right. I'll say this. No nasty surprises last night, with you on duty."

Peter glowed with the praise. "Here you are, sir. Fresh and hot."

"Thank you, Peter. Though I sure wish we had a bowl of spoon cream to drop some in it."

A happy grin of remembering brightened Peter's face, making him look even more likely to be thirteen than seventeen. "Yeah! I remember . . . remember back when Paw was at home and we had that thick, sweet cream. I liked to put spring-house chilled peaches in it in the summertime. An' Paw'd let me take a sip of his coffee." Peter caught himself babbling and vulnerable and arrested his runaway tongue. "Ah . . . nothin' but fatback and beans for breakfast, Mr. Clutter."

"That's good enough, Peter. You know, you sort of remind me of my boy when he was your age."

"I—I do? Gol-lee, Mr. Clutter," Peter blurted, then turned away to keep the older man from seeing the unmanly tears that welled up in his eyes.

"We're gonna catch up to Baylor today, or it'll be too late. Crow agency isn't more than forty miles from here," Clutter informed the youth.

"Then we go after the Caldwell woman?" Peter inquired, eagerly.

"That's right. Only, after that bungled bank holdup, my guess is that she's not too far away. Might be we'll get a double before sundown."

"That'd be nice. Then I could go on my way, right?"

"Lane and Al see it differently," Clutter reminded him. "For my own part, I'm not interested in riding with this bunch. Too many amateurs."

Peter looked at the ground, scuffed a boot toe. "Meanin' me, huh, Mr. Clutter."

"Not in an unkind way, Peter. You should find somewhere to settle down, try a hand at a trade or working a ranch. As far as the others are concerned, you may not think you've measured up, but you're all right by my book. We've a duty to our kin. After that, a man's got a right to choose what he wants from life. Don't you forget that."

"I won't, Mr. Clutter," Peter promised solemnly.

* * *

"That's him, by God if it ain't," Al Honeycutt declared as he lowered his field glasses. "I'll swear on it, Mr. Clutter. Lone Wolf Baylor, sittin' that Palouse horse against a screen of trees. Bold as brass he is, too."

"Do you think he suspects anything?" Lane Tulley inquired of no one in particular.

"I think he's one clever son of a bitch," Loomis Clutter replied. "Could be he's leadin' us on. Naw. That can't be. We've not cut any sign other than his so far. All right, boys. We split in two groups, swing wide and come at him from two sides. He won't have a chance."

Ten minutes later. Loomis Clutter wondered what had given him the idea Baylor didn't know of their presence. Moments before the two wings of his outlaw army were ready to close on their target, Baylor turned his horse's nose and walked off into the trees. When they got to the spot, they found no sign, other than a few bent and broken pine needles or smaller branches. Clutter sent Al Honeycutt and Matt Wellington to scout along the spoor.

"Let's ride," Clutter commanded as he put away his gold-cased turnip watch. "He's got a ten minute lead on us. Anything happens, we want to be close enough to fall on Baylor before he can get away."

Without warning, the screening trees ceased to offer concealment some twelve minutes later. A wide, bowl-shaped meadow lay before the avengers. Near the center of the grassy depression, Honeycutt and Wellington could be seen, heads bent, eyeing the ground for more sign as they rode along. Beyond them, Clutter could see the mouth of a narrow valley.

Movement alerted him and he pointed, after a moment's verification. "There. There he is, the son of a bitch. He can't get away in there. Let's go at him full tilt."

In brief seconds twenty sets of hoofs flashed as the gang raced pell-mell across the meadow. Calmly, Lone Wolf sat his Palouse horse, eyeing their approach. When they came within forty yards, he reined to the right and trotted off into the valley. Giving a shout, Loomis Clutter thundered after him.

Lone Wolf glanced back and smiled with satisfaction when he saw the galloping outlaws. His heels touched Thunderer's ribs and set the animal to a faster gait. Already the enemy had crossed half the space separating them from him. A little further. Then, like Crazy Horse, as a boy of twelve, he would close the trap on this modern day Fetterman, and see how he liked it.

"Kiii-yiiiii-kii-yii!" From twenty-four Crow throats, the chilling war-cry sounded over the valley, echoed off the rock-strewn walls and once more assaulted the surprised and frightened outlaws.

"What the hell . . ." came a muffled exclamation from Loomis Clutter.

"Jesus! Indians!" Paddy O'Toole shouted.

"A whole hell of a lot of Indians," Raymond Dawson wailed as he attempted to spur his horse off in the opposite direction.

"Hail Mary, full of grace . . ." Niel Mallory recited,

his Irish brogue thickening with each word.

Ahead of them, Lone Wolf whirled his horse and came charging back, a Winchester to his shoulder, throwing round after round at the shocked whites. Out front, and isolated from any help, Loomis Clutter and Peter Dillon saw a beautiful woman in Indian dress riding toward them from one side and a Sioux warrior approaching from the other.

"Get back, Peter. Go!" Clutter commanded.

"But, Mr. Clutter . . ."

"Do as I say, Peter. I'll hold them off. Looks like Baylor and the Caldwell woman outsmarted us. Run for it, Petey!" His voice had close to a pleading tone.

"I can't leave you alone, Mr. Clutter," Peter said stubbornly.

Bullets snapped past their heads. Horses shying, and powder smoke drifting between them and their attackers, Clutter glanced at all sides. "No need for you to die, Petey. Go on."

"You come too. We'll fight 'em another time," Peter said stubbornly. When he received no answer, he reached for Clutter's reins. Fixing them in his hand, he gave a hard yank and spurred his mount.

"They're getting away!" Whirlwind shouted over the tumult.

"Time to play our trump," Rebecca yelled back as they closed on the spot where Loomis Clutter and Peter Dillon had been moments before.

"What does that mean? 'Trump?' " Whirlwind asked, baffled by the alien English word.

"Have our Oglala attack," Rebecca explained. She

raised in her stirrups and blew into a buffalo-horn trumpet.

Wild and eerie, like the wail of the highland pipes, a breathy note sounded over the shattering noise of battle. It hooted and moaned, fading off to a lingering suggestion of sound, then ended. Most of the outlaws, those still living, raced toward the mouth of the narrow valley. To their great horror, they came close to their expected safety only to see a force of twenty-seven Oglala warriors, in the blue Army shell jackets and kepis of the Indian Police rise up in their path.

With a rippling crash, shots spat from twenty-seven Springfield .45-70 carbines. Five outlaws spun, fell or flipped backward off their mounts, mortal wounds already spilling their life-force to soak into the red-brown soil. Horses shrieked and squealed as six went down, legs shattered or intestines punctured. One took a 405 grain slug in the left eyesocket. Instant brain turn off splayed its surging legs and its immediate collapse sent the rider hurtling over its head.

Tall and graying at forty-one, a victim of the uniformly slow promotion in the frontier army, Captain Walter Westmorland answered the summons to his commander's office at Camp Robinson, some thirty miles south of the Black Hills, in Nebraska. Westmorland cut a handsome figure, in or out of uniform, and as a widower was considered a prime catch by single ladies from Baltimore to Omaha. His most recent assignment had been to Fort Meade, a liaison officer to the Department of the Army. When his transfer to the west came through, without the coveted promotion, he became bitter and suspicious.

Did he have enemies in Washington, determined to sweep him under the advancement rug and let him get forgotten on the frontier? Had he done something wrong? Whom might he have offended? Suspicious by nature, and petty in his resentments, Westmorland never once considered his change in assignment came because he had served long and well as a cavalry officer and officers of that branch, with experience, were desperately needed out west. Only the prospect of action, of a chance to even the score for those he knew who died with Custer, urged him to take the change without complaint. Once he arrived at Camp Robinson, he made a concentrated effort to fit in.

His success toward this end he would soon discover as he entered the colonel's office and reported with precise formality.

"At ease, Walter," Colonel Parsons responded. "Take a chair."

"Thank you, sir," Westmorland responded. "The colonel wished to see me, sir?"

"Indeed. Walt, I have an assignment for you. One I'm sure you're going to like a great deal," the CO informed him.

Westmorland tugged on the left side of his full, flowing mustache. "Yes, sir. What is that, sir?"

Parsons stroked his clean-shaven chin, berry-black eyes twinkling over his full, generous lips: "A deputation of miners, prospectors and small businessmen from the settlements in the Black Hills has been to see me. They are highly concerned over recent outbreaks of lawlessness and violence. Men have been killed, stores and assay offices robbed, all of which they blame on the Sioux. The Oglala tribe in particular. They have demanded that something be done. Civilian law is incapable of handling the widespread disorder. The Army, and you in particular as its representative, has been prevailed upon to look into the matter and quash any Indian uprising. Your company is to be outfitted and prepared to leave here by tomorrow morning, following Officers' Call."

Slowly, though he tried to suppress it, a great, beaming smile spread on Walter Westmorland's face as he rose and saluted. "Yes, sir. I'll begin preparations immediately, sir. We'll find who's at the bottom of this and smash them sir, you can count on us."

"Excellent, Walter. I expected you'd be enthusiastic over this prospect. Carry on."

"Yes, sir!" the eager captain fairly shouted.

Through the growing dust, Rebecca saw a frighteningly familiar face. *Jake Tulley!* No, her reason told her. It couldn't be. She had watched Jake Tulley fall into the fiery shaft of a grain silo in Kansas years ago. Then she remembered with icy clarity. The prisoners they had questioned in Farmingdale had mentioned a brother, Lane Tulley.

Over the calamitous roar of the battle, she uttered a mighty shout. "Tulley!"

Thinking it one of the gang, Lane Tulley made a signal in acknowledgement and looked around. His eyes fixed on Rebecca's angry visage and he paled slightly. At once, the determined young woman forged her way toward him.

He fired wildly, a sinking feeling overtaking him as

he saw her continue to force her way through the melee. Once more Tulley threw a shot at Rebecca and turned his horse in desperation, seeking a way, any way, to escape from the howling Indians and the certain death they represented. Most of all he wanted to avoid contact with the angry woman pursuing him.

Rebecca had her own idea about that. She dodged a rider who put himself between her and the outlaw she sought. Dust and powder smoke swirled past, obscuring her vision. When she could see again, Tulley had disappeared. Quickly she scanned the battle, hoping to find him. Could it be that he had already fallen? She urged *Sila* forward, the screams of wounded and dying men sharp in her ears.

"Becky, look out!" Lone Wolf's voice shouted from a distance.

Rebecca bent low over her horses's neck and heard the distinct crack of a bullet as it went through the space occupied by her chest only a moment before. With a hard yank on the reins, she turned *Sila* in the direction from which the slug had come. Faintly she made out the shape of Lane Tulley's body. Afoot now, he had crawled into some boulders and brought fire on the frenzied fight below him. Feeling like a fly on sticky paper, Rebecca worked her way to an edge of the conflict, determined to circle out of Tulley's view. If she could accomplish that, she could finish off her enemy.

Only a few yards from her goal, three rapid shots tore the air close around her. One bullet grazed *Sila's* haunch. Although well trained and accustomed to war, *Sila* lost his tenuous control because of the hot pain in his rump. Feet bunched, the Palouse stallion

154

began to crow-hop, squalling and farting, he spun one way and the other, until at last he managed to dislodge his rider. Rebecca sprawled in the pulverized grass while *Sila* bolted off in an attempt to escape the hurt. Quickly she rolled over and came to her knees, a Smith American at the ready.

She located Lane Tulley as he rose slightly from his nest of rocks. Winchester at his shoulder, he took careful aim at a spot between her eyes. Rebecca fired first.

Her bullet showered Tulley's face and eyes with fine chips of rock and bits of lead. Before he could recover, Rebecca shot him again, in the chest. Her third round entered his belly. Lane Tulley went rigid a moment, then fell slackly among the boulders. Still worried for her safety, being on foot, Rebecca looked around for a horse.

Sila stood shivering in a growing space of calm. With a start, Rebecca realized that those outlaws who hadn't been killed or severely wounded had managed to escape. Gradually silence settled on the battlefield.

"That's over." Lone Wolf's voice echoed in her head.

"Yes," she said lamely. "It is. Now . . . now we have to reorganize and go after those girls in the bordellos. I want to put Lotta Crabtree out of business for all time."

155

Chapter 15

Major Harvey Storey looked up from his paperwork at the clatter of many shod hoofs. It couldn't be the Ridgeway woman, he decided. The Oglala warriors who rode with her didn't shoe their horses. Boots thumped on the roofed-over porch, followed by a brisk knock.

"Come in," Harvey Storey commanded.

A tall, lean officer, hair showing gray at the temples, entered. "Captain Walter Westmorland, sir," he announced. "Colonel Parson's compliments, sir, we've come about the Oglala uprising."

This announcement astonished Harvey Storey as much as if the captain had announced that hostilities had resumed in the Civil War. "What are you talking about, Captain Westmorland?"

"Why, the Oglala raids into the Black Hills, sir," Westmorland replied.

"Nonsense. There's been no such thing," Storey boomed. "I can account for every man, woman and child at this agency."

"I'm sure you can, Major Storey," Westmorland said rather smugly. "But the fact remains that the miners and businessmen in Deadwood City and other parts of the Hills have stated that the Oglala have been raiding, so, of course, they have been."

Anger touched Major Storey, not so much at the sneering slight of his administrative ability as at the glaring sophistry of Westmorland's bland assurance that because someone had said it was so, it had to be so. Controlling his ire, he determined to set the misinformed officer straight.

"There are thirty-one children between eight and fourteen years of age at the mission school at Pine Ridge. Two women are in the hospital with ailments. Twenty-nine of our Indian Police are conducting an authorized investigation into the stealing of children. To date, eleven boys and girls have been abducted from this agency. All others are, and always have been, present."

Westmorland looked sincerely regretful. "I'm sorry, sir, but that's not the way it is. Perhaps you have been lax in keeping track of the savages. Warriors from your Red Top Lodge band have been slipping off the reservation and attacking innocent whites in the Black Hills. They're considered sacred to the Indians, you know, sir," he concluded condescendingly.

Storey could no longer contain himself. "I know a goddamned lot more about it than you do, Sonny. I was at Fort Phil Kearny when Fetterman met his end. Still there in sixty-eight when we pulled out and the Sioux burned the fort. I served with Crook in seventy-six. And took my retirement to open this agency two years ago. Your reasoning, that if a white man said it about an Indian, it has to be true, is as flawed as Aunt Hetta's one-legged rooster. And about as pro-

ductive. I suggest you leave the management of Indians to those who know something about it. If the
Army has to put in an oar, why not investigate the
taking of Indian children from five agencies, and the
possibility that white criminals might be responsible
for the robberies and murders?"

Westmorland's contempt blazed from his face.
"How utterly preposterous! Perhaps you have, ah,
'gone Indian,' living among them for so long, Major?"

"I've no more gone Indian than Mrs. Ridgeway,"
Storey snapped.

"Ah, yes, Mrs. Ridgeway. Colonel Parsons has
some questions he'd like to ask her, also. Where might
I find her?"

Harvey Storey felt a coldness touch his heart. "Well,
ah, she's not here at the present. One of the children
taken from here was her son. She's with the expedi-
tion searching for them."

A bright glow suffused Capt. Westmorland's face.
"Is she now? A half-breed and nearly thirty Oglala
braves out running around the country? Where, do
you know, have they centered their so-called investigation?"

Even more miserable, Storey lowered his head and
spoke in a subdued tone. "In the Black Hills."

"Aha! Thank you, Major Storey. You've just provided me with the proof I sought. There's no question
now but that a renegade half-breed woman and a
dangerously large number of warriors from this
agency have started an uprising that is costing hundreds of white lives. We'll set out at once to run these
miscreants to earth and exterminate them. The leaders, I'm instructed, are to be taken back to Camp

Robinson to be hanged. Good day, Major. In the future, I'd suggest you keep a closer eye on your charges."

Scarlet-faced, Harvey Storey didn't wait until Captain Walter Westmorland reached the porch. His voice held the bellowing quality of an enamored bull. *You unprincipled BASTARD!"*

"Where do we go?" Peter Dillon asked in a tone of confusion and despair.

"The Black Hills, I suppose," Loomis Clutter responded. "How many of us made it, Petey?"

"Maybe fourteen. They're scattered all to hell and gone." Right then Peter discovered for the first time that his bladder had let go during the fight.

Misery added to his mingled emotions. How the gang would rag him now about being a little boy. No, they wouldn't, his waning shred of confidence told him. He'd stood his ground beside Loomis Clutter and fought their way out, while so many others had run away.

"We've a long ride ahead of us. Maybe we'll gather some of them up along the way."

"What are we going to do in the Black Hills?" Peter inquired.

"I've a feeling Baylor and the Caldwell woman will come hunting us. We'll have one more chance at getting our due."

A frown creased Peter's high, smooth, youthful forehead. "I'm not all too sure I'm up to getting any more revenge, Mister Clutter."

To his surprise, Loomis Clutter found he could

laugh. He let it boom out, drawing a startled look from Peter Dillon. "I'm not so certain I am either," he said between guffaws. "But if they do come after us, we had better be ready, Petey."

Joey Ridgeway put down his spoon in the silence of the night. Even the everpresent cicadas remained silent. Joey rightly suspected a heavy thunderstorm was not far away. Holding his chains to keep them quiet, he slid over closer to Tommy Archer.

"*Mahtolasan,* Mule-Ear Johnson is sort of all right. He does what he can for us. You've seen that. Red Tyback's another matter. He's mean and stingy, and sometimes he can't keep control of his hands — if you know what I mean?"

"Yeah. The other day he took a lot of interest in whether I had rock galling in my crotch. Made me wonder."

"That's what I mean . . . only it isn't just that. We've got to escape soon or we'll never be able. We're workin' harder, but we're getting weaker. I know it. So we have to be ready when the time comes. Badger and *Pangeca* are giving up. I'm afraid they might try to make themselves die if we don't have some hope of getting away."

"You mean like Moon Son af-after his beating?" Tommy asked in a choked voice.

Joey nodded. "So, help me think of something fast."

Within four days, eight of the original avengers had banded together. Matt Wellington had come in first.

160

Then Ike MacKinnon, Raymond Dawson, Sheldon Boyle, Niel Mallory, and Nathan Pierce had been located or came to their camp over the next two days. Each had his own tale of the battle and their escape. All agreed Lane Tulley had died at the hands of Rebecca Caldwell. By the evening of the fifth day after the fight in the valley, they stopped for the night within sight of the brooding, rounded black hills they sought so desperately.

"We'll be there tomorrow. Then what?" Matt Wellington asked in ill temper.

"Find a stake, a safe place and wait it out," Clutter answered curtly.

"You can't come up with anything better than that?" Matt demanded.

"What would you suggest? We've seen enough indications along our back-trail to know they're coming after us. Alone none of us would have a chance," Clutter laid it out.

Grudgingly, Wellington agreed. "That leaves us damned little choice."

"We can make them come to us. That's what we should have done in the first place. Somehow they all got ahead of us and took the initiative. This time we turn the tables. I'll set a watch schedule and we can turn in, get an early start."

Being surrounded by the pine-covered mountains gave Peter Dillon a closed in feeling. His nerves twitched and the common sounds of squirrels, birds and insects made him jump. By mid-afternoon of the next day they came upon a small mining camp. Twelve men worked three holes at the site and gathered eagerly to hear news of outside.

When Clutter and his men had satisfied the miners' curiosity Loomis asked, "What's new around these parts?"

"The Army's out," a blocky, bearded specimen informed him. "There's been lots of killin' and robbin' and such. Army says it's the Sioux an' sent a piss-and-vinegar captain out here to hunt them down. He passed through here yesterday. Said them Sioux were raidin' as far west as the corner of Montana not even a week ago."

Clutter and his companions exchanged meaningful expressions. Somehow their involvement had been kept out of it. They felt more at ease.

"There's supposed to be a white renegade ridin' with them. A woman if you can believe that. This Captain Westmorland says he's gonna hang 'em all when he catches them."

"Now, that's my kind of soldier-boy," Matt Wellington exclaimed heartily. Smiling broadly, he drew his sixgun and killed the talkative miner.

Acting as if it had been a signal, the rest of the gang produced weapons and cut down the other men in camp. Sheldon Boyle went around dispatching any wounded with a bullet in the back of the head.

"We ought to make a nice haul out of this," Matt Wellington observed as he and the others began to strip the miners of their valuables.

"More'n a couple of pounds of gold here," Ray Dawson remarked, a greedy glint in his eye.

"Injuns wouldn't take the gold," Loomis Clutter told them. "If we want to stir up more trouble for our friends behind us, we'd better not either."

"Awh, Mr. Clutter," Dawson began to protest.

162

"I said we leave it and ride on. We've yet to find a safe place to lay for Baylor and Caldwell."

Lashing his mount wildly, a young trooper rode up to the column of blue-uniformed men. His salute was reckless at best. "Captain, sir, we come upon an awful sight up ahead. Whole lot of miners been killed and left to the elements, sir."

"Slow down, trooper. How were these miners killed?" Captain Westmorland asked.

"Shot, sir. From what we could tell. Bloated pretty bad, and gnawed on by animals. Terrible messy, sir."

"Sergeant, bring the column forward at the trot. I'll go ahead with this trooper and look things over."

"Yes, sir, Captain. Right away, sir."

Ten minutes later, Walter Westmorland wished he hadn't been quite so impetuous. Black and green bloated corpses littered the ground. Fewer than four remained whole. All stank terribly. He started to gag. Most of the men had used their yellow neck scarves to cover their faces. Steeling himself, Westmorland dismounted and bent to examine the closest body.

Gunshot, all right, he assured himself. Not scalped either. Not a sign of an arrow or a broken lance. It didn't fit with what he had been told at Camp Robinson. No doubt the renegades had become better armed. He straightened and paced a few yards with hands behind his back.

"It's the Sioux for certain," he declared. "Those damned Oglala. No doubt safely back on the reservation by now."

Westmorland stopped speaking as the company

trotted into the clearing. He exchanged salutes with the first sergeant. "Sergeant, I want a burial detail. From what I can see, it's the Sioux. I want you to send a messenger to the outpost at the Pine Ridge Agency. Have the man convey my request for artillery. We'll ride to the Rosebud reservation and shell the Sioux encampment until the criminals are handed over to us."

Although the Big Bertha mine employed a lot of people, the settlement up a branch canyon from the main gold strike area could support only a single bevy of soiled doves. Naturally, the house belonged to Lotta Crabtree. Thirty gamblers crowded the main saloon, drinking, gambling and fondling young women. Giggles, squeals and an occasional shriek caused by a pinched bottom escaped into the night. With them came the disjointed notes of an upright piano, played inexpertly by a thoroughly intoxicated maestro of the ivories who had recently become a victim to the onset of arthritis. The bartender, who could take on any three miners no-holds-barred and win, stuttered and had a harelip. He also stole from the till. The Silk Garter was indeed the garbage pit of Lotta's extensive operation.

It also won the distinction of becoming the first bordello to be visited in Rebecca's effort to fire the Sioux girls. Shortly after midnight, the front doors flew open, glass shattered in the windows and the patrons found themselves looking into the muzzles of rifles competently held by copper-skinned Oglala braves. A few bows, they noted, also put in an appearance. When one of the miners took exception to this interruption, he received an arrow in his shoulder for his courageous vocal defense of Lotta's property. Rebecca entered a moment later, a Smith American held with casual expertise in her right hand.

"We've come for the little ones. The Sioux girls you have here."

"I don't know what you're talkin' about, *Honey*," the aging whore who functioned as madam declared in a brassy voice.

"You'd better find out fast, *Honey*," Rebecca informed her. "Or I'll put a bullet hole where that black patch beauty mark is located." The muzzle of Rebecca's .44 Smith indicated the heart-shaped pasty high on the snowy globe of the whore's left breast.

"You wouldn't dare do that," the hard-eyed harridan challenged.

"Don't try me," Rebecca stated grimly. "Search the place," she ordered in Lakota.

Five warriors edged further into the main salon of the bawdy house and spread out. Two who went upstairs soon returned with a trio of sloe-eyed Sioux girls, dressed in frilly white woman's frocks.

"That's all," Hawk Slayer informed Rebecca.

"Everyone listen closely. You have five minutes to clear the building. I want everyone out. There will be no exceptions and no delays. In exactly five minutes we are going to set this place afire. Anyone left inside will die here. The time begins . . . now."

"Say, who are you, anyway?" the madam demanded. "Lotta's gonna make you pay something awful for this."

Rebecca snickered in her face. "When you see her, please tell her how worried I am."

Five minutes later, to the second, the fire began. Amid the curses of the miners and the wails and lamentations of the turned-out whores, Rebecca and her followers rode off with the rescued children.

Chapter 16

Pine knots crackled cheerfully in the fire, located well back in the cavern-like excavation on an east-facing slope of the tall bastion the white men had already started calling Mount Rushmore, after an early explorer and engineer. At Lone Wolf's recommendation, Rebecca and Whirlwind chose this location for their retreat, where the girls taken from Lotta Crabtree's brothels would be brought until the rescue operation had been completed. Rebecca gnawed the last flesh off a squirrel leg, tossed away the bone and licked her fingers clean.

"What about the boys?" she asked of the three Yanktonai girls removed from the Silk Garter.

Subdued and ordinarily timid, the barely pubescent Sioux girls hesitated answering. At last, one raised a hand and waggled nail-bitten fingers. Rebecca nodded to her.

"This many boys came with us from the agency," Bright Leaf spoke in a near whisper. "One died on the way. The men who stole us traded the boys to the men who dig in the ground."

"To the miners?" Rebecca questioned.

"Yes. Those who want the yellow metal."

"Where was this?"

"To the south of where we entered the sacred hills," Bright Leaf explained.

"Did one man take them all?" Rebecca queried.

Bright Leaf shook her head. "No. One time a man took a boy, Rabbit Nose. Another place a man took two boys, Fat and White Legs. The other boy they kept after we went to that awful place."

"Would they have traded the other boy?"

"We don't know. We didn't understand their words." Bright Leaf provided apologetically.

"This was only the start," Rebecca remarked to those gathered around. "From each girl we take from this Lotta Crabtree, we will learn something about more of the boys. How I wish someone could make a map, showing each location."

"I may be a Talks to Spirits now," Lone Wolf put in, sounding a little hurt. "But I can still draw a map. Let me trace in the shape of the Hills and see what the girls can tell us from that."

"It will take days," Rebecca objected.

"Like you said, this won't be the last raid," Lone Wolf reminded her, searching for materials to begin his task.

Tiny wisps of smoke still spiraled upward from the ruins of the brothel that served the Big Bertha mine. Angry, sullen miners stood in clusters around the soldiers who surveyed the scene. Arms crossed over his sunken chest, Capt. Walter Westmorland strode back and forth, listening to the excited babble of the madam and her girls.

Ordinarily, he would look with disdain on such examples of society's dregs. His duty demanded, however, that he treat them with consideration, if not respect or as equals. The older, shop-worn hooker had drenched herself in some absolutely abominable scent.

"You say they were definitely Indians?" Westmorland asked, breaking the cataract of their emotional recitations.

"Oh, yes, your honor, er-ah, Captain, sir," the blowsy madam gushed.

"*Sioux* Indians?" Westmorland pressed.

"Oh, I wouldn't know that, your hon—, Captain," the reeking chief whore answered.

"I'm certain we can safely assume they weren't Apaches? Or Blackfeet, or Crow?"

"Oh, there was some Crows there. I recognized them from their headdress."

Anguish crumpled Capt. Westmorland's face. *"They were Sioux!"* he bellowed in her face. "Oglala Sioux, to be exact. You must have seen that clearly, now didn't you? Remember, Miss, ah, Trudeau, the accuracy of your report will have a large bearing upon whether the government compensates you for your loss."

Her mother may have raised up a few hookers, Lilly Simms, aka Monique Trudeau, reasoned, but she didn't grow any stupid ones. Her expression changed to one of eager avarice. "Oh, yes, yes indeed. I see it clearly now. They were Sioux right enough. Like you said, Oglala Sioux."

"Be-Jazas," a grizzled cavalry sergeant muttered to

his friend, Owen Clancy, "T'a little shit's leadin' them whooers around by their quims right enough."

"Naw, Terry-me-boyo, tiz by their pocketbooks he's leadin' 'em." Owen answered.

"Thank you, Miss Trudeau," Westmorland said with a sigh of relief. "Now then, have any of you, ah, ladies something else to add?"

"There was a woman with them, giving the orders, in fact," a seventeen year old prostitute, fighting a losing battle with acne, announced.

"A . . . *woman?*" Westmorland asked archly. "Think carefully and describe her for me, please."

"Ummmm. Well, she wasn't too tall. Not mannish or anything. About my height, good body, nice looks. In our business she could make a fortune. But she wore Injun clothes," the soiled dove wrinkled a nose reddened with pimples.

"A squaw dress?" Westmorland prompted.

"Sort of. It was made of skin. White, with rows of beadwork and fringes. Her hair was black and done in braids. An' she had blue eyes. Spoke English too, like a normal person."

"Aha!" Westmorland exclaimed loudly and tritely. "Rebecca Ridgeway. I knew it. She's reverted to type. A renegade. What reason, if any, did she give for burning your, ah, house?"

"It was over them . . ." she started.

"Babette!" Monique Trudeau yelled sharply.

"Aaah, she, ah, didn't say," pimple-dotted Babette finished lamely.

"I think we have what we need, gentlemen," Westmorland announced delightedly as he turned to his two junior officers. "First, Sergeant, see that this is

170

written down in proper form later. As of now, I'm issuing a shoot on sight order for the person known as Rebecca Caldwell Ridgeway, a half-breed renegade. She, and the band of outlaw savages she leads, is guilty of murder, mayhem and arson."

"Sir, ah, begging the captain's pardon, sir," one of the junior officers stammered, "but I don't think . . ."

"That's right, Lieutenant, you don't think. Situations like this are the stuff that promotions, comfortable postings to Washington City or the Academy, and brilliant careers are made of. We will find Ridgeway and her heathen killers and make an example of them."

"Sir, I . . ."

"Just think, Lieutenant. Before long, you may be commanding this company, while I—I'll think often and fondly of you while I sip a julep on the verandah overlooking the Chesapeake Bay, after a hard day at the office." Westmorland's voice turned hard. "See that my orders are carried out."

Bullets shattered the large mirror behind the bar of the Variety Hall in Dog Town. Shrieks and wails came from the frightened soiled doves who clustered around potential customers. Two miners drew weapons, to their regret. A hot slug shattered one's forearm, while the other took an arrow in his thigh. While he writhed on the floor, five Sioux warriors entered through both front and rear doors. Four of the ten broke off at once and climbed the stairs two at a time.

From above came the indignant brays, terrified squeaks, and harsh profanity of the girls disturbed at

171

their work. Only a minute passed before the first of these started down to the main salon, their bodies covered by whatever articles of clothing or bedcovers they could snatch before being forcibly ejected from their cribs. Two of the braves appeared at the top of the steep stairway with big-eyed, confused Indian girls at their sides. Already, those with keen hearing could discern the hungry crackle of flames on the upper floor.

"Everyone out," an incongruously blond Indian demanded in perfect English. "We've set the place on fire. Down here is next. No delays."

"You say you want a job, dearie?" a small, rosebud mouth in a snow-field face of makeup and mascara inquired.

Across the low table and tea service in the parlor, the raven-haired beauty in the revealing dress leaned forward, nodding enthusiastically. "I'd be ever so grateful. I really need it."

"You'd do well, I'd judge. Lotta has to make the final decisions. But for me, you can start tonight. You have any preferences? Or, ah, kinks?"

"N-no. I don't under— Oh, you mean like would I refuse to work with a person of another color. Like the Indian girls."

The lumpy, middle-aged woman interviewing her narrowed her eyes. "Where'd you hear about Indians?"

Her visitor shrugged. "Around. A lot of the miners think I do a great show. Like mother and daughter. I like to do that."

"Well, we've got four of them here. Chances are

you'll get a chance," the madam told her confidently. "Not letting Lotta okay you is takin' a chance, but get your things together and move in this afternoon. You can go to work tonight."

"You're taking an even greater chance if you don't do exactly what I say," Rebecca Ridgeway informed her as she withdrew her hand from the black, beaded reticule, exposing her .38 S&W Baby Russian.

"What is this?" the madam demanded, certain she knew only too well what had happened.

"Speak when I tell you to. First off, I want you to summon those Sioux girls. Bring them here, without a guard," Rebecca commanded.

"You'll not get away with this. Lotta will have your hide."

Rebecca smiled sweetly. "She hasn't so far. Next, to return to our subject, when the girls are brought here, and we are alone, just the six of us, I want you to pick up that flower pot and throw it through the window. That will be the signal for my followers to move in. Everything will move rather rapidly after that, so I would suggest you come with us, to avoid being hurt and stay outside while we do what's necessary."

Mouth working in consternation, the madam finally formed words. ". . . —an't get away with this in broad daylight."

"Oh, but we can. You see, I've taken the time to inform the local law of your practice of holding minor children in bondage. Mr. Creighter might not have official recognition, but he does wear a badge and he's angry enough right now to have you all hanged from the nearest tree. So I suggest your total cooperation will be of benefit to you as well as to us. Go on now, be a good girl and call for the children.

Wearing a shiny star, pounded out of the first substantial nugget discovered in the Big Bertha strike, Marshal Wendall Creighter studied the younger man in the blue uniform of any army officer. He massaged his clean-shaven chin and thought of what the pretty young woman had shown and told him. He liked her pluck, danged all if he didn't. Now this feller, with his sandy-brown hair, watered down blue eyes and perpetual mean grated the wrong way. Sort of like trying to eat a lobster with the shell still on. His last remark had decided Creighter.

"Eh — yep. We had a fire here, right enough," Creighter stated in his flat, Down East twang. "Burned it to the ground. Only it weren't Indians who done it, howevah."

"And I'm telling you it was. Oglala Sioux and Crow warriors, to be precise, led by a woman named Rebecca Caldwell Ridgeway," Captain Walter Westmorland snapped.

Creighter pursed his lips, more in suppressed mirth than in an effort to conceal his lie. "It appears you haven't spent much time out here. If you had, you'd know that the Sioux and Crow would nevah ride together. They're traditional enemies. More to the point, you couldn't get a warrior to let a woman lead him to the suppah table, let alone in battle."

"They're riding with the Ridgeway woman," Westmorland snapped. "I have put out an order to 'shoot on sight' on her, in the name of the Army. Anyone who harbors her and her accomplices, or aids in their

174

evading capture, is subject to the same penalty. Now what do you have to say?"

"I'd say you have a mighty terrible medical problem for an army officah. You haven't heard a word I've said. I'd check into that if I were you, young fellah."

"Don't get insolent with me, *Mister* Creighter," Westmorland warned. "Or I might just go ahead and have you shot."

"That's Maw-shel Creighter, Captain. And I wouldn't be considerin' that proposition too seriously, considerin' all the miners standin' around heah with their rifles. Now, good day to you, sir."

Wind whipped around the corners of buildings and moaned down the long, single street of Deadwood City. The few street lamps flickered wildly and cast weird images in the fitful shadows. Under an ancient, gnarled oak at the edge of town, Rebecca Ridgeway met with Lone Wolf, Whirlwind, Stone Breaker and Two Owls for the final briefing before they made their raid on Lotta Crabtree's central operation in Deadwood. The tree had become known as the Hanging Tree, because most of Deadwood's miscreants met their end on a rope, strung over one of its long, stout branches. A fitting place, Rebecca thought, for what they had in mind.

"We know from what Lotta's 'managers' told us that there are seven girls in this one place. We will have to hold all entrances and the persons inside long enough for a search. It's a big place, three stories at the center line. What we don't know is where the girls are kept. My guess is that they will be in small cubicles in the attic. There's a cellar, too. It's used for storing and cooling beer. Chances are they won't put the girls there, unless as punishment for one or two who get out of line. We have a lot to do and little time to accomplish it."

"What about the people outside?" Lone Wolf inquired. "The customers, too, for that matter?"

"It's the same as before. If they leave us alone, they won't get hurt. Once we have the girls free, we can go to the local law. Sheriff Moulton, I've heard. With the evidence we present him, he can take it from there."

"And what do we do with Lotta?" Whirlwind asked.

"We can turn her over to the sheriff if she tells us who the men are who stole the children. Otherwise," Rebecca went on grimly, "we can take her with us and turn her over to the mothers of missing children."

"How can anyone with so warm a heart be so cold?" Whirlwind wondered.

"I'm half-Sioux, remember?" Rebecca riposted. "The important thing is to get answers. Another thing, we can't burn this place down, due to the wind. A big fire could get away and burn the whole town. Now, we had better go get the warriors and take up position."

Twenty minutes later, an accidental explosion deep in the Homestake mine brought the residents of Deadwood out into the street in worry and alarm. After five minutes of speculation over the sudden collapse of two laterals and a gas explosion, their distress changed to panic when twenty Sioux and Crow warriors, painted for war, rode into town.

People fled in all directions. The cry of, "Injuns! We're under attack!" went up all along the wide,

176

perpetually muddy thoroughfare. In the midst of the disorder, two drunken residents managed to knock a street lamp from its post. Kerosene in the reservoir splashed the wall of a tent saloon and flames soon crackled up the canvas. In the confusion created by this blaze, another fire ignited inside an empty eating house. Whipped by the wind, they soon started a general conflagration.

While the pandemonium raged, Rebecca and her followers struck their blow at the Crabtree Social Club.

Chapter 17

"Fire!"

"Injuns!"

The chilling words, shouted from outside, galvanized the patrons and inmates of Lotta Crabtree's brothel to instant, and varied, actions. The girls, not presently engaged with a customer in one of the cribs, raced screaming for the stairs. Like frightened birds, they went up, not down. Some of the men joined them, while others drew weapons and started for the doors. Before they reached them, the portals slammed open and the Indians they sincerely hoped weren't really outside put in an appearance.

Crow braves at the back, Sioux warriors at the front, with more covering the side entrance to Lotta's private office, Rebecca and her rescuers stormed the bastions of sin. Lotta had risen from her usual place, a plush booth at the rear of the establishment, at the first outcry. She carried a large, beaded reticule and had thrust a hand inside.

When the raiders entered, she withdrew her hand,

178

holding a short-barreled Colt .45. Hardened to life in dangerous places, she coolly took aim and shot an Oglala warrior in the chest. He lurched forward two steps, caught a bullet from the bartender and crashed to the carpeted floor. At once, the less timorous of her customers took up the battle.

Gunshots crashed from all quarters and the strings of Sioux and Crow bows twanged musically to the launching of a half dozen arrows. One struck the barkeep in his paunchy stomach and he howled in agony as he dodged below the mahogany for its scant protection. Rebecca appeared in the doorway and blasted out a pair of suspended kerosene lamps. In the sudden dimness, both sides developed poorer aim. Lotta took a shot at Rebecca and found herself under murderous fire from the Smith American the elkskin-clad white squaw aimed her way.

At once, Lotta bolted for the door to her small office. A hot lead pellet smacked through the upper panel, beside her head, as she managed to turn the knob. Fear propelled her quickly inside. There she double-bolted the portal and pressed her back against the dividing wall. To her chagrin, she found herself gasping, throat dry, hands trembling. From outside she heard the conclusion of the brief battle as the last defender died. Where was Will Hardesty and his men when she needed them so badly? She threw the fragmentary question aside when the doorknob rattled violently.

Two bullets through the center ended the present threat. Wild thoughts cascading, Lotta tried to make sense out of the raid. Through the cooperation of local lawmen, outraged at her use of children in her bordellos, she had been isolated from any knowledge of the previous attacks. Now she sought both a reason and a means of escape.

Cautiously she went to the side door and peered out a small peep hole. Three painted warriors stood with backs against the neighboring building. Her bolt-hole had been effectively stoppered. What to do? Part of her answer came in the sound of loud pistol reports. The lock case shattered and some heavy object struck the center of the door.

Reflexively Lotta recoiled from the danger and fired her last shot. With fumbling fingers, she groped in a desk drawer for loose cartridges with which to reload her sixgun and recalled the ejector rod had been sacrificed to the two inch barrel. Moisture streamed from her armpits, droplets formed on her upper lip. A stray strand of her fading carroty hair fell over her left eye. She brushed at it impatiently and the two rounds she held went flying across the room. A slintering crash jerked her attention around to the door.

Split in half vertically, the thin portal swung inward ahead of the bench four Indians used as a ram. Rebecca Ridgeway stepped through the wreckage. Lotta examined the woman in the Indian clothing and realized that she, too, had fired her last cartridge. Instantly the aging madam launched herself at the younger woman.

Hands drawn into talons, sharp nails flashing, Lotta slammed into Rebecca and sought to tear her flesh. Rebecca dodged the dangerous fingers, took a back-step, and delivered a solid punch to Lotta's midsection. Lotta uttered a strained, "Oooph!" and tottered back two paces. She blinked and came to her nemesis once more.

"Stop fighting," Rebecca grunted out as she evaded Lotta's attempts to maim her. "We've taken your place. All we want is to have the names of the men who sold you those Sioux girls."

"You can go . . . to . . . hell, you breed . . . bitch!" Lotta spat as she swung her fists in uncoordinated assaults on Rebecca's body.

Rebecca stepped in and delivered a solid back-hand slap to Lotta's right cheek. It staggered the madam, yet far from ended the conflict. Lotta shrieked in rage and snatched up a book from the end table. She hurled it and charged.

Ducking, Rebecca avoided the volume of Dickens and tripped her opponent. Lotta sprawled on the floor and tried to kick Rebecca in the crotch when the white squaw dove at her. Rebecca turned and took the pointed toe on the outside of her left thigh. It hurt like the torments of hell, and required conscious effort to shut out the ache. Lotta grabbed one of her braids. When the violent madam yanked, Rebecca went with the force, rather than resist it. She banged her forehead into the bridge of Lotta's nose, then inched forward until she could close her mouth over the now-throbbing appendage.

Lotta screamed in genuine agony when Rebecca bit her nose. Her body flopped up and down and her legs

181

flailed the air. Rebecca held on, one hand attempting to extricate Lotta's hold on her hair, the other gouging a thumb at the madam's right eyesocket. An exquisite jolt of blue-hot pain radiated through Lotta's body and, with a soulful sob, she ceased to struggle.

"You barbarian bitch," Lotta blubbered. "I'm ruined. Ruined."

Lone Wolf gave Rebecca a hand up and motioned for Whirlwind to take charge of Lotta. Once Rebecca had arranged her clothing and ceased gasping for air, she crossed to a table and set an extinguished lamp upright. Locating a match in a small hand-painted china dish, she struck it and lighted the coal oil fixture. Then she gestured for Whirlwind to bring Lotta to her desk.

"First, I want the names of the men who sold you those Indian girls. Then I want their descriptions. After that, you can give me a written confession of your involvement in this slave operation, naming the men again and details of when they brought you new captives."

"I'll not give you anything, you Indian-loving slut!" Lotta spat, her rage renewing.

Smiling pleasantly, Rebecca drew a thin-bladed skinning knife from her belt sheath. Yellow lamplight sparkled off its keen edge in a blue dazzle. Still smiling, she stepped close to Lotta. "You think you're ruined now. What if I took this and slit your cheeks from the corners of your mouth to the jaw hinges? Or cut your belly open just a little bit and let your intestines slither out on the floor?"

182

Lotta could never be accused of not having a vivid imagination. She began to tremble and tears leaked down her face. Her lips formed soundless words of pleading.

"Cooperate and you can avoid all that," Rebecca hurled at her. "Who were they?"

"W-w-w-w-w . . ." Lotta began, totally unbalanced. "Wi-Will Hardesty. He's the boss. And there's, ah, Ed Miller, Nehemiah Logan, Vic Parks, Norm Watson. That's all the names I know."

"What do they look like?" Rebecca demanded, inwardly relieved she didn't have to come up with more threats or to distastefully begin to carry out one already made.

Haltingly, eyes fixed on the dreadful knife in Rebecca's hands, Lotta described the gang members. When she finished, Rebecca pointed behind the desk.

"Sit down and write all of that out. Start with the first time Hardesty came to you. List dates and number of girls you took in, what happened to them. Write it all out and sign it."

Like an automaton, Lotta Crabtree walked behind her desk. She fought to keep her face neutral, to show no sign of the wild last hope that bubbled in her mind. She sat in the familiar chair, then reached for the top drawer.

"There's a pen and paper in here," she explained.

"Get it," Rebecca commanded.

Obediently, Lotta opened the drawer and reached inside. She came out with a small .41 Remington rimfire derringer. Her shot cracked in the quiet of the room a moment before Rebecca hurled the knife.

The stubby, underpowered, conical bullet from the .41 rim-fire cut through the elkhide on Rebecca's left shoulder and split the skin. It caused a hot, throbbing, painful wound, but did little damage. Rebecca's knife, on the other hand, had struck Lotta in the chest. The long, slightly curved blade slid through the lower portion of her left breast, between two ribs and lodged in the main artery of her body.

"We can do nothing more here. Let's get going," she commanded.

"All of the girls are safe," Whirlwind reported, also avoiding the gory sight on the desk. "Two of them say they know where *Pinspinzala* and *Mahtolasan* were taken."

Joyful anticipation filled Rebecca after a moment in which a catch in her throat almost convinced her that her heart had stopped. Forging ahead of the others, she started out of the ruined bawdy house.

"Where are they?" she implored. "I have to talk to them right away."

Joey Ridgeway lay curled tightly into a ball on his blanket inside the mine entrance. Beside him, Tommy Archer sat staring listlessly out at a steady downpour. Behind them a short ways, Badger and *Pangeca* lay on their backs, breath shallow, as though in a stupor.

"What can we do, Joey?" Tommy asked miserably.

"I don't know. They've stopped eating. I'm afraid they'll just lie there and will themselves to death. You

184

know, I used to think that sort of stuff was the bunk, when I was a white kid. Now . . . well, I just *know* that it works."

Tommy brightened, cheered by something for the first time in days. "Joey, did you hear what you just said?"

"Huh?"

" 'When I was a white kid.' Joey, you're thinking Indian, just like I started to do. You're really *Pinspinzala* now."

Joey pushed out his lower lip in a pink pout. "Lot of good it does. With *Hoka* and *Pangeca* giving up and all, what I wonder is how long can *we* take it?"

"'Least we don't have to worry about a beating. We're covering for them, aren't we?"

"For how long?" *Pinspinzala* asked frankly. "I'm sore and tired all the time. We both work like crazy people to do their share and ours, too. If they got whipped, or we all did, I just know it would be like with your friend."

Grief dimmed the glow in *Mahtolasan's* eyes. "We're not supposed to speak the names of the dead. But I miss him so. He was a good friend."

"What *can* we do, *Mahtolasan?* We've tried . . . everything."

"We can talk to them," *Mahtolasan* suggested. "Try to keep them listening, so they stay here with us, instead of . . . slipping . . . away."

Pinspinzala brightened. "Why not tell them funny stories about *Śica* and *Putehin?* And maybe some of the lessons the medicine man tries to teach us about being brave and growing strong?"

Mahtolasan frowning considered it. "It's worth a try," he agreed brightly.

"Boys, this is the last time we're gonna go after any redskin brats. Once we deliver our catch, we're off to see them Dutchies," Will Hardesty informed the men seated around the green baize table in the Sure Shot saloon in Spearfish. "We'll ride to Whitewood, take the train to Rapid City, then cut south to Pine Ridge. Then we can grab us a dozen or so Sioux kids, haul 'em up around Rockerville and The Needles. We take our money and head to Rapid City. From there we take the train, the J.R. Haggin'll pull us and our horses all the way to Pierre and it's an easy ride from there."

"How much are you countin' on making?" Ed Miller asked.

"All the traffic will bear," Hardesty disclosed with a chuckle. "We'll want to whoop it up a little in Pierre before starting after them white-haired Dutchies. They grow big, strong boys and those broad-hipped gals are regular humpin' machines from what I hear. Not anybody up in the Hills wouldn't want to buy a couple of them. Drink up, we've a long haul to make."

Rebecca and Lone Wolf, dressed in their white man's clothing, entered Spearfish, acting on information provided by Lotta Crabtree. The mining commu-

186

nity had the usual bustle and hell-raising of its sister cities. Saloons outnumbered all other enterprises and remained open around the clock. They had raided a whorehouse here earlier and the local law knew of their mission. Even so, it was a risky prospect to spend too long around the hard and rowdy miners whose pleasure palace they had so recently destroyed. An inquiry at the marshal's office brought a suggestion they should visit the Sure Shot saloon.

"Nope," the bartender asserted. "Never heard of 'em."

Rebecca described Will Hardesty and two others with exacting detail. Again the apron shook his head and denied any knowledge with a bland expression he sincerely believed would convince the Pope himself of his veracity. It only served to convince Rebecca he lied through his teeth. She finished her glass of wretched sherry and Lone Wolf downed a beer. On the way out, a disreputable old man in a ragged coat, with the wet, slobbery lips and rosy nose of a habitual drunk accosted them.

"Uh-uh-you was a-a-askin' 'bout Will? Will Hardesty?" he stammered, eyes beyond them, fixed on the amber glow made by shafts of sunlight striking bottles on the backbar.

"Yes, we were," Rebecca responded, not entirely taken by their new companion.

"Uh-uh-I, uh, know him, Miss. Know 'em all. Will, an' Norm Watson, an' 'Miah Logan. If uh-uh-you, er-ah, was to buy me a, ah, drink, I could tell you all about them. Wh-wh-why'd you ask about th-them

187

fellers in th' first place?"

"We were supposed to meet them here," Rebecca answered, then produced a five dollar gold piece from her small, lady-like purse. "If you tell us all you know, we'll see you can buy a whole lot of drinks."

"Wh-why, thank-ya ma'am. M'name's Louie. I'm o-ob-obliged. M-mind if I get one right now?"

"Go right ahead," Rebecca invited.

"Whiskey, Harry. An' I want the good stuff. I got money, Harry. Say, ah," he went on, casting a glance back at his patrons as if for approval. "Make it a bottle, eh, Harry?"

Louie returned in a moment with a bottle, hugged to his chest like a precious gem, and one glass. He slopped the contents badly when he poured. With an appreciative sigh, as though a connoisseur of fine wines, he downed the glass. Smacking his lips, he poured another, with considerably less difficulty, and restrained his urge enough to make two swallows out of it. Then Louie seated himself, added more whiskey to the tumbler before him, clasped his quaking hands and looked his patrons straight in the eye.

"First off, to be, ah-ah, honest, I have t-t-to tell you that they're gone. They were here, the whole bunch, only they left."

"Do you know where they went, Louie?" Rebecca inquired.

"Yep. Said something about Rapid City, an' on to Pine Ridge. What'd they want to go to an Injun reservation for?"

"I think we know already, Louie. Did they say they

188

might come back here?"

"Naw. Talked about goin' on to Pierre an' some place called Dutchie."

"Thank you, Louie," Rebecca said sincerely as she started to rise. "I'll give you another five dollars if you promise to spend it on food, not whiskey."

"Oh, I sure will, Miss. Sure as I'm born'd," Louie responded solemnly, his hand lifted as though taking an oath. Visions of four full bottles lined up side-by-side danced in his head.

Chapter 18

Brightness filled the whole world. Birds sang, the sun shone brightly, puffs of cottony cloud dotted the sky, as though in celebration of their enormous success. Will Hardesty and his crew rode along in a jolly mood. Their sweep of the fringes of the Pine Ridge agency had netted them an unprecedented sixteen youngsters from ten to fourteen. They had heard of the strange circumstances of raids on Lotta's whorehouses and refrained from taking girls, who would provide little market. The boys, sullen and subdued after a few cuffs and punches, rode three to a horse, bound tightly together. The calvalcade topped a low rise and ahead spread the vista of the Black Hills. Unseen by the triumphant child stealers, angry eyes intently watched their progress.

"That's them," Lone Wolf declared, lowering his field glasses. "They have about sixteen boys with them."

"There's no better time," Rebecca suggested.

"Why don't we pull back of that knoll and line up

across their path?" Whirlwind suggested. "They won't expect to see any Sioux ahead of them. The surprise might defeat them better than bullets."

"Good idea," Rebecca agreed.

Eight minutes passed while the rescuers lined up like a formal war party. Each Oglala had removed his blue shell jacket and kepi and replaced them with the regalia of Sioux warfare. Their Crow friends had also painted and primped for battle. Twenty minutes went by before the slave train approached a sentinel set out by Stone Breaker. His hooted signal alerted everyone and they put on their grimmest faces.

Over the rolling prairie the outlaws rode, talking loudly as they rounded the knoll. A moment later they stopped abruptly. Never, in their worst of fevered dreams had they encountered so terrible a sight. Fully thirty-five warriors faced them, fully armed, feathered, painted and ready.

Uncertainly, Will Hardesty raised his hand in the peace sign. "How!" he greeted. *"Kola,"* he said next, using the Lakota word for "friend."

Big Ears rose in his stirrups and waved his bow above his head. *"Hu ihpeya wicayapo! Huka hey!"*

"Wha—what did he say?" Ed Miller queried.

"Something about them whippn' us real bad, then bendin' us over and fuckin' us in the rear," Norm Watson said in a sinking voice.

"Oh, Jesus," Nehemiah Logan moaned.

"Maybe we should have called on Him sooner than this," Victor Parks suggested. "Those fellers look like they mean it."

"Let them kids go," Ed Miller suggested. "Maybe they won't bother us then."

"I wouldn't bet more'n a dime on that," Hardesty said softly. "Draw your irons, fellers. If they charge us, we'll let the brats go, open up with all we've got and ride like hell right through them. Maybe they won't chase after us then."

"I've heard of it workin' like that before," Ed Miller urged.

"We ain't got a hell of a lot of choices," Norm Watson offered.

"Oh, Lord have mercy, *here they come!*" Nehemiah Logan shouted.

Vengeance bound and not the least interested in taking prisoners, the Oglala warriors flew across the prairie sod. Clods of dirt and grass flew from their ponies' heels. Filled with the confidence that *Wakan Tanka,* the Great Spirit, watched and approved of what they did, they fearlessly charged the seven unmoving men who aimed rifles at them.

Those Winchesters cracked and four warriors slid from their horses, mortally wounded. Still, on they came. Here a tomahawk caught the brightness of mid-day sun, there a bow sang mournfully and a shaft sped to imbed itself in the front haunch of a horse. The rider cried out in alarm and struggled to hold on. His intense concentration on staying upright continued until a Sioux bullet shattered his skull.

"All right, let's ride!" Will Hardesty commanded.

After another volley, the outlaws spurred forward, allowing their captives to turn away and fend for themselves. The two lines clashed and men shouted curses in two languages. Dust rose and obscured the brief violence. Then the white men broke free. Wiping grime from their eyes, they trotted forward some twenty paces before they looked up . . .

. . . And saw another file of Indians facing them, Crow this time.

"Oh, Christ have mercy!" Nehemiah Logan wailed. "We're goners for sure."

"Quit prayin' and start shootin'," Will Hardesty suggested sharply.

Spurring their mounts to a gallop, the remaining six charged the Crow. Only to be attacked in the rear by the Sioux. Horses shrieked and reared, men screamed and died. Realizing that there would soon be no one left to question. Rebecca fought desperately to end the killing. When she succeeded, only three had managed to escape and they had but one prisoner live.

"You fought well," Whirlwind told the prisoner.

"He says you fought well," Rebecca told the surprised man. "Your friends are all dead," she exaggerated slightly. "You might as well tell us where you took those boys. If you don't do so willingly, I'll turn you over to the fathers of some of them. Two of them are right here with us."

"Oh, shit," Norm Watson moaned. "You got me dead to rights, ma'am. Who are you, anyway?"

"I'm a special agent for the Rosebud Agency director. We've been trying to catch you for a long time."

"You've caught me, but I'm not saying anything."

"Oh, I think you will. You see, I'm also the mother of one of the stolen boys."

Watson paled and swallowed with difficulty, remembering the two tow-headed boys they got at the Rosebud. His resolve melted like August snow. Further coercion unneeded, he nearly babbled as he named as many mine locations and owners as he could remember. When he finished, Norm Watson resigned himself to dying a horrible death.

"We have wounded who can take him back to Major Storey," Rebecca observed. "While they do, we'll start out to free the boys."

"Do you remember the time Coyote set out to make man walk on all fours, like he must do?" *Pinspinzala* asked, beginning another story.

"Do we have to?" Badger complained, his voice suddenly stronger than in several days. "We've heard it so many times. Why not tell us one of the fun stories the older boys tell each other, about making the eight-legged creature with Sunbeam or Gray Faun."

Joey's gaunt face brightened, and his eyes sparkled with enthusiasm. "It worked!" he squeaked in English. "Badger wants to hear dirty stories," he went on to *Mahtolasan*.

"What's the matter with you? Talk so a person can understand you." Badger protested.

"See?" Joey went on in Lakota. "He's himself again. A grumbler, like always. You've been sick, Badger," he

194

explained. "Now you must eat and get strong again."

"I want to go home," the young Oglala pleaded.

"We will. First you and *Pangeca* must eat and move around some. Don't ask me how I know that," he added when Badger started to interrupt again. "I just . . . know it."

Early morning light fell across the clearing around the Tyback-Johnson claim. *Mahtolasan* produced food from a cache the boys had created and fed the previously unresponsive youngsters. While they munched on chewy sourdough bread and cold meat, the transformation of returning strength was almost visible. *Pangeca* got up and began to pace the anteroom of the mine entrance. His restlessness transmitted to the others. Although the boy remained in a weakened condition the others found it no surprise when he began his bending and twisting routine. In scant minutes, he stood before them, free of his chains.

"Put them back on," Joey hissed. "If they catch you, they'll whip you."

"But I want to go now," *Pangeca* argued.

"We could do it," *Mahtolasan* agreed. "Today's Saturday," he continued, using the English word, then repeating it in Lakota as they thought of it since their captivity. "It's Go-to-town-and-get-drunk day."

"We have to plan," Joey countered.

"We can, until they leave," *Mahtolasan* assured him. "Then we can get free and be on our way."

"How will we get food?" Joey asked worriedly.

"Think like an Oglala, *Pinspinzala*," *Mahtolasan*

chided. "We can snare rabbits, get fish on the way. Enough to keep our strength."

Joey—*Pinspinzala* again, now that his excitement had begun to ebb—contented himself with that for the present. He led the discussion of what they would take from the mine and what course they would follow after leaving. The talk continued, covertly, through breakfast and until the miners had made ready to leave for town.

"There's plenty of food, boys," Mule-Ear Johnson informed them when he came to the mine at the last minute. "We're only going to Alder Gulch, so we'll be back tonight some time. Red ain't gonna like this, so don't come out until after we leave. I'm gonna put you on the long chain leads so you can get to the crick and wash off some, an' move about under the trees."

"Thank you, Mule-Ear," *Pinspinzala* responded, lowering long lashes over his eyes in a properly submissive manner.

"You boys be good now, hear?" the grizzled miner admonished.

Thirty minutes after the men departed, the escape attempt went into motion. *Pangeca* slipped his bonds entirely and went about searching for a hammer and cold chisel. The best he could come up with was a single-jack star drill. That turned out to be badly in need of refacing. They had their work mauls to drive it, yet another problem faced them. They could not cut the rivets that held the bands around their waists. It would be necessary to cut a link of the chain and take with them the symbols of their captivity.

196

Under enthusiastic pounding, the iron links spread slowly, parted at last, leaving first Badger, then *Mahtolasan* and finally, *Pinspinzala* free. Quickly they made up travel bags. Cornmeal, sugar and meat figured high on the priority. After long, soaking baths in the icy creek, they were able to put on loincloths and moccasins. With all in readiness, they took a final look at their place of torment and set off toward the treeline.

"I thought I'd better check back," Red Tyback snarled as he entered the clearing. "You little bastards are too smart for your own good. I've learned me some Sioux talk over the years and it put me wise to you along before breakfast. Now you're gonna pay."

Tyback uncoiled his bullwhip and flexed powerful muscles in readiness to strike one of the boys. Before he could, *Pinspinzala* hurled a melon-sized granite chunk that struck the brutal miner in the side of his head. With a grunt, Tyback went to his knees. Instantly the four boys swarmed over him.

Nearly six weeks of terrible confinement guided their anger as they used fingers, teeth and any object that came to hand. Beaver, who had been most severely whipped, got hold of the bullwhip and used its braided, sinuous body to wrap around their tormentor's neck. With silent determination, he began to strangle Red.

Meanwhile, the others stripped the clothes from the nearly comatose Tyback. *Pangeca* brought a shovelful of dirt from a near-by ant hill, containing hundreds of painfully biting red ants. This he dumped on Tyback's

197

bare, pasty-white belly.

"What if Mule-Ear comes back?" *Pinspinzala* asked of a sudden.

For a moment the boys froze. Then Badger released his strangle knot. Immediately, Tyback began to scream hoarsely from the torment of the ants. On the ground, less than three feet away lay his cartridge belt, holster and sixgun. *Mahtolasan* walked over to it. He picked up the heavy Remington revolver and returned to the writhing man. Earing back the hammer he pointed it at Tyback's chest.

The .44 made a loud roar in the confines of the canyon. Red Tyback flopped like a landed fish, terrible groans coming from him, while blood splashed everywhere. *Pinspinzala* grabbed the revolver from *Mahtolasan*'s numbed hands.

"You didn't do it right. He's still alive," *Pinspinzala* criticized, nearly choking on the bile that rose in his throat.

He took careful aim and squeezed the trigger. Then he flushed with embarassment for having forgotten to cock the hammer. This he did and aimed again. The Remington spat flame, smoke and noise and a black hole appeared in Red Tyback's forehead.

"Let's get out of here," *Mahtolasan* urged, running shaking fingers through his cottony hair.

"Get his horse," *Pangeca* suggested, eyes wide and stomach aboil.

"Two up and two running, we'll make good time," Badger observed.

"Yes. Until we can take more horses," *Mahtolasan*

198

agreed.

"Quick, before Mule-Ear comes," Badger urged.

Within three minutes, the boys had their bundles loaded on Red's horse, with the two Oglala boys mounted, while *Pinspinzala* and *Mahtolasan* ran alongside. It took no time for them to disappear.

From the cover of the trees, at some three hundred yards distance, Mule-Ear Johnson watched their departure. He absently made a swipe at a tear that ran down his cheek. He'd not shed it for his former partner, for whom he spared little affection. Over the days and weeks, he had come to like those little buggers. Now he'd miss them, for sure.

Rain threatened by mid-afternoon. Fat, lead-bellied clouds had moved in over the Black Hills and brought an unnatural hush to the creatures of the area. A swift, chill breeze whipped the pale leaves of cottonwood and aspen, made soughing sounds through the pine boughs. In the distance, lightning split the sky. Capt. Walter Westmorland felt decidedly unmilitary as he repeatedly blinked his eyes to rid them of tiny bits of vegetation that whirled on the face of the growing wind. Although he would never admit it, this big, empty country intimidated him.

It seemed exaggerated in every proportion. Even the rain came in tumultuous storms. The fierce lightning would fry the life from man or beast with the same indifference it blasted and charred random trees. His brooding on the weather brought him to the source of his most immediate discomfort.

Walter Westmorland didn't like in the least the civilian contingent that had attached itself to his command. Loomis Clutter seemed an all right sort, and the boy, Peter, was . . . fetching. The others appeared to him to be little more than brush-poppers and border riff-raff. Nine of them. Said they were a citizens' posse, looking for the same people his detachment pursued. Perhaps so. He would see as time went on. Now he directed his attention to the galloping figure of one of his advance scouts, returning in haste to the column.

"Sir," the breathless rider reported with a hasty salute. "Corporal Jenkins' compliments, sir. We've come across something unusual, sir."

"Such as what, Trooper?" Westmorland asked dryly.

"Four boys, sir. Sioux boys. They're all mounted and have a pack animal. Two of 'em's got hair white as can be. Headed across our course, sir. Corporal Jenkins thinks they're bound for the Rosebud Agency."

"Well, well. That *is* a find. White hair, eh?" Westmorland turned in the saddle. "Sergeant, take six men and ride those renegades down. Perhaps we can wring some answers out of them."

"At once, sir," Sergeant Richter snapped. "Parsons, Brown, Hoffman, Cunningham, O'Mahoney, Terrant, fall out of ranks and come with me."

"Pony soldiers," Badger called out, instantly tense and distrustful.

200

"They're coming after us," *Mahtolasan* stated a moment later.

"Don't we want them to find us? They can help," *Pinspinzala* inquired.

"Pony soldiers *never* help," Badger admonished him.

"Then we run for it," *Pinspinzala* whooped.

Heels drumming their mounts' sides, the four boys raised to a gallop and streaked toward a distant canyon. They covered some fifty yards when the first fat drops fell from the sky. Long, forked fingers of raw, white light seared across the horizon and a momentous thunder clap jarred the earth. While it rolled away through the hills, *Pinspinzala* heard the flat pops of weapons discharged behind them.

"They're shooting at us!" he shouted. "We've got to get away."

"In there," Badger cried, pointing to the canyon mouth. "It twists and turns and we can climb out along somewhere and they'll never find us."

Chapter 19

Warm raindrops spattered on the pale white corpse in the clearing. Will Hardesty, Ed Miller and Victor Parks stared in fixed revulsion. The flash and crash of the thunderstorms added to the eerie drama of the scene.

"Jeez, that's mighty awful," Ed Miller said in an awed tone.

"It's the Injun kids. They're rising up against the ones who bought them," Parks declared.

"That was Red Tyback. One tough feller," Hardesty said in sincere tribute. "How'd they ever get the best of him?"

"It don't matter now, does it, Will? If they get any more free, and the word gets out, our lives ain't worth a nickel," Miller stated.

"You've a point. We'd better track these boys down and finish 'em," Hardesty decided. "Then come for the others."

Most of the trail left by the escaping lads led under heavy trees and had as yet to be wiped out by rain. For two hours the survivors of the child-stealing ring made fast time, covering a lot of ground. Nearing the eastern fringe of the Black Hills, the signs became sketchy where the storm had washed away hoof prints and covered other indications of the boys' passage.

"Look over there," Ed Miller called out twenty minutes later. "All that churned up mud. Those kids didn't do that."

"Let's follow that trace a ways and see what we find," Will suggested.

To their good fortune, Will and his fellow outlaws spotted the Army before the rear guard of the column saw them. Wisely they skirted wide and checked the ground as the slow-moving storm wore itself out and left the sodden hills behind. It took them little time to mark new tracks headed into the canyon.

"It's the ones we've been following," Will stated confidently. "We go in after them. Chances are we'll be safe from this threat right soon."

"They got away from us in the storm, Captain," Sergeant Maitland replied to Westmorland's angry question.

"I won't tolerate excuses, Sergeant," Westmorland snapped, as he paced the confines of his tent.

"I understand, sir. When the rain hit, the visibility dropped down to a couple of feet. All trail sign got wiped out. Beggin' the captain's pardon, sir, but we had no way of following them."

"Very well, Sergeant Maitland," Westmorland concluded with bad grace. "Did you get close enough to have a good look?"

"Yes, sir."

"And what did you see, Sergeant?"

"Well, sir, two of 'em were Sioux, right enough. The others . . . well, they had light hair and sort of the look of white boys. About twelve or thirteen I'd judge, sir. But they had braids, and were all but naked, in loincloths and moccasins, just like the Sioux."

"Renegades, by damn. Like I suspected, Sergeant."

"If you say so, sir," Sgt. Maitland stated glumly.

"Didn't I tell you, Captain?" Loomis Clutter injected.

Clutter had been fidgeting since camp had been set up early for the night. He felt sure that at least one of the white boys would be related to Rebecca Caldwell, and might serve to draw her out where they could get a shot at her.

"Yes, you did, Mister Clutter," Westmorland answered icily. "And in light of events, what would you suggest we do about it?"

"You seem to have found the answer already, Captain. Declare the white boys renegades. Hunt them down. Then use them to find the woman leading the real band of raiders."

"Ummm. You pose an interesting course of action." Westmorland stepped over to a field case and produced a dusty bottle, half-filled with good bourbon. He poured a tot for Clutter and himself and handed the outlaw boss his glass. "To a swift conclusion. The boys are obviously renegades, as you said. We'll pursue them relentlessly and interrogate them with zeal. Then . . . then we shall hang them."

Micah Strand awakened to the cool touch of a knife

204

tip to his throat. Blinking he started to struggle, only to have strong hands press him back against his rude cot in the little shack next to his mine. The voice that spoke to him came out clear and icy.

"Nothing to get excited about. We're relieving you of the two boys you've held as slaves. Sorry, no compensation for your loss, and if you object too strenuously, we'll slit your throat."

After the midnight visitors had departed with his two workers, Strand could swear that the person who spoke to him had been a woman.

Daylight brought a hail of lead into the clearing around the Diamond Stickpin mine. Rudolph Zanger, the owner, dove for cover and missed the sight of seven Sioux warriors, a blond man in Crow war regalia and a young woman rushing toward the small shed where he chained up his Indian slave. He saw them at last and raised up with an angry bellow. Zanger's hand snatched at a Parker shotgun, which he leveled at the bold-as-brass folks who would rob him of his property.

That effort earned him three arrows in the back. Twitching out his life, he flopped on the ground while the rescue party faded off into the trees. Before leaving they had retrieved the arrows and didn't even scalp him.

Blasting powder boomed deep in the First Strike mine. Two crouching, coppery-skinned boys looked up to see the familiar faces of their tribe. The leader spoke in Lakota, while the rest fanned out to located the white miners.

"Do you know of any boys from the Rosebud Agency? Two of them have white hair?"

"No," the youngsters answered simply.

The answer had been the same everywhere. When the miners were frog-marched into the clearing, bound with rawhide thongs, the Sioux warriors looked them over in contempt.

"We should leave you like that to starve," one who spoke English told the frightened white men.

He looked about and found a butcher knife on the slab of pine used for food preparation. Hefting it, he turned back, then flung it across the open space.

"You can go after that when we leave," he said flatly.

"It can't be that they weren't sold to one of these miners," Rebecca stated with a hint of uncertainty. "The girls in Deadwood told us they had been sold to someone. A one-eyed man with a red beard."

"We'll keep looking," Lone Wolf told her.

"Of course we will. But . . ." Rebecca's determination silenced her doubts.

Half an hour's ride, with a growing number of Sioux boys stringing along behind, they came to another mine. A fresh grave had been dug and a man sat alone near it, swigging from a glazed clay jug. At their approach, he looked up and waved.

"C'mon in. Red's dead. Done for by those boys he bought, though I can't blame them. I'm Mule-Ear Johnson, Red's partner. I came back to dig him a hole. You lookin' for the kids, they took off to the

206

east. It's gonna be mighty lonely around here without Red. Mostly without them, though. I, ah, hope you get 'em safe to their folks."

Through his speech, Rebecca could barely contain herself. Now she blurted out, "Joey was here?"

"Mule-Ear sprang to his feet, his crushed hat held before his chest. "That's right, ma'am"

"I'm—I'm his mother," Rebecca stated quietly.

"May the Good Lord have mercy on me," Mule-Ear muttered, eyes downcast.

"You treated him well. At least as best you could. I can tell," Rebecca told him gently. "There's good in you, Mule-Ear Johnson. We'll not begrudge you the opportunity to find that out. How long ago did they escape?"

"Yesterday. Before the thunderstorm. I marked their tracks, Headed almost due east, like I said. Good luck to you, ma'am"

"And to you, Mule-Ear," Rebecca concluded.

Although frightened, the miner readily spoke up while being relieved of his captive laborers. "That's right, ma'am. This soldier-feller has a shoot on sight order out on you. It would be best you steered clear of the Hills for a while."

"Thank you, Mister Eckert. I'll keep that advice in mind, Rebecca told him.

Once away from the mine, Rebecca reined in and spoke tightly to Lone Wolf. "Let's find the Army and get this straightened out."

"Isn't that the worst thing we could do right now? We don't want someone trying to kill you," Lone Wolf protested.

"On the other hand, if the Army doesn't rescind that order, every man in these hills will be gunning for me. After we find the Army, we can figure out how to get it stopped."

Their small band came upon the military camp an hour before sundown. Careful scouting determined the strength of the detachment and that none of the missing children were with them. They had followed intermittent tracks from Johnson's mine that indicated Joey, and whoever was with him, had come this way also. One point of interest immediately caught Rebecca's attention.

"Some of the men who sought Lone Wolf are in the camp," Whirlwind informed her. "I know their faces."

"That makes this a bit more difficult," Rebecca reflected aloud. "The officer in charge is obviously the one who issued the order on me. How do we get him alone long enough to convince him that he made a mistake?"

"We could go in and take him away from his soldiers," Whirlwind suggested with a smile.

After due consideration, late in the night, Rebecca, Lone Wolf and Whirlwind set about putting his idea into effect. Silently they slid past the inattentive sentries and slipped through the sleeping camp. When they came to the right tent, they waited a long while until satisfied his snores were genuine. With the greatest of stealth, the trio entered through the front flap. Tensely they gathered around the cot, looking down at the slumbering officer. At a nod from Rebecca, Lone Wolf and Whirlwind moved swiftly.

Their combined strength proved far overwhelming

to Captain Westmorland. Despite his struggles, they had him gagged and bound in minimal time, without any alarm sounding. Now came the hard part; getting him out of camp without arousing the company of soldiers.

"Through the back," Rebecca suggested, her sharp knife separating the canvas.

With careful steps, the two men carried Captain Westmorland away from his quarters. He lurched in their arms, in an attempt to created enough noise to attract the sentries, until their steel grips pained him severely. In the star-glow, the line of trees could be seen fifty paces away. Past that point, they would encounter no problems.

"Post number four, all's well. Relief in thirty minutes."

"Post number five, all's well. Relief in thirty minutes."

Guards called off their stations as required by routine. The first one to sound off had nearly panicked the abductors, who shrank into the shadows with their unwieldly burden. When the ritual ended, Rebecca led the way forward. Twenty feet from shelter, a soldier's voice sounded from uncomfortably close at hand.

"Hey, is that someone out there? Speak up!"

"Only me, soldier," Loomis Clutter replied. "Had to go relieve myself."

"You should stay inside the perimeter sir," the guard informed him.

"Sorry. Next time I will."

Rebecca regretted greatly that she daren't take the opportunity to put a bullet in Clutter's head. With a sigh of relief, the small group reached the trees. In seconds they became only more of the dark shadows that menaced the camp in silence.

"What is the meaning of this?" Capt. Walter Westmorland demanded an hour later.

"We wanted to present you with some overwhelming evidence, Captain, before you made a regrettable and irreparable error," Lone Wolf informed him.

"I don't understand you. What error, what evidence?"

"We have in our camp here some thirty girls and boys, stolen from their homes by an organized band who sold them into slavery in the Black Hills. These youngsters happen to be Sioux, but the law is the same. Slavery is a federal crime, forcible abduction is also a crime. You have issued an extraordinary order regarding a woman who has been most active in seeking those children. We hope to convince you of your mistaken purpose in this."

"How do you propose we do that?" Westmorland sneered, totally unconvinced, and certain he would remain so.

"Talk to the children. The girls were sold to a madam named Lotta Crabtree. The marshal in Deadwood is holding her now for the circuit court. The boys were made to work in the mines. One of them, who is still missing, is the son of Rebecca Caldwell Ridgeway, the woman you ordered shot on sight."

"The renegade white boy! I see it now. And these savages with you?"

"Are carrying papers, and wear the uniform of Indian Police. They, and Mrs. Ridgeway were duly authorized to conduct an investigation into the disappearance of children from the Rosebud Agency. Listen to the children, Captain. No one can hear their stories without being deeply affected."

An hour later, with dawn threatening in another cycle of the clock, Walter Westmorland came away from his interviews with the former captives. His face had become ashen, but not in fear. Anger seethed within him. He had never heard of such horrid things done to children, all in the name of making a profit.

"The men responsible for this must be made to pay," he said tightly.

"They have already been severely punished. All but three or four, who escaped us. When we find them, they will die."

"And you'll have my thanks for it," Westmorland said sincerely. "Now, about this Ridgeway woman . . ."

For the first time, Rebecca revealed herself. "Yes, Captain, what about me?"

"I—ah, that is, er—ah, apparently I acted under misinformation. I will rescind my former order immediately, of course," he added regretfully. How he hated ever admitting to being wrong. "You seem to have something else on your mind."

"I do," Rebecca said straight out. "You presently have a number of men in your camp who are responsible for most of the crimes you attributed to me and the Indian Police. Loomis Clutter and a Peter Dillon, to name two." Quickly she explained the series of crimes committed by the gang, and the purpose behind them. When she finished, Westmorland had a sickly look. He'd been gulled again.

Striking a palm with his fist, he looked about for a horse. "We had better get back there quickly, then.

Again, Mrs. Ridgeway, my apologies. Will you be coming with me?"

"I feel sure you are competent to deal with a few bungling outlaws, Captain. Our little group here are setting out to find Joey and his friends."

Chapter 20

A slight chill hung over the Black Hills as evening came on. When Ed Miller slipped from his saddle, he could seen steam still rising from the dropping he had bent to examine. A confident smile creased his face.

"Not an hour away, Will. You sure called this one right."

"We have to stop those boys, Ed. Everyone keep your guard up. They're Indians and tricky. One slip that lets them know we're around and they'll disappear like smoke."

Darkness began to slip into the deeper contours of the Black Hills by the time Will Hardesty and his companions located the campsite where Joey and the other escapees rested for the night. Vic Parks edged forward on his belly and studied the layout until the youngsters yawned, stretched and rolled into blankets. Soundlessly he slithered back to where Will and Ed waited.

"They're all there, right enough, four of 'em. Sound as bugs in a dung hill. Should be sound asleep by now," Ed summed up.

"Good a time as any," Will declared grimly. Then, with a tone of anguish, "Goddamnit, I don't like the idea of killin' kids."

"We've got to do it," Vic Parks reminded him. "You said so yourself."

Quietly the trio edged forward under the trees and around a bend in the hill. No sign of a fire showed. It took Ed Miller five minutes of careful searching to locate the exact spot. Breathing heavily, through his open mouth in an effort to be silent, he reported his success.

"Make it quick and clean," Will Hardesty commanded. "I don't want them suffering."

The three outlaws had to splash through an icy stream to reach the boys. Gingerly they entered the water, which rose to knee depth and flooded their boots. On unsteady footing they made the crossing and climbed onto the opposite bank. They had squelched forward some three feet when a figure rose out of the dark shadows and fired point-blank at them.

Pinspinzala and his friends enjoyed their freedom, yet kept conscious of the need to put miles between them and the Black Hills. Another day's ride would put them far out on the prairie, crossing familiar land. After a meager supper, they rolled into blankets and settled down to sleep. At least the soldiers would not find them now.

* * *

Moving quietly into position, careful not to betray their presence, Rebecca and her most trusted followers worked their way to within twenty yards of the sleeping boys. Each had found a place around their banked fire, feet inward, lying out like the spokes of a compass or a sundial. How she wanted to rush to Joey and hug him. Yet there existed the quite real presence, close at hand, of the men who had stolen them in the first place. Despite her argument to the contrary, it had been decided that this was the best way to insure the boys' safety and capture the last of the child stealers. She tensed as she heard soft movement in the brush to one side, near the stream. A moment later she saw three dark figures rise up and wade into the water.

Carefully she took aim with her cocked and ready Winchester.

Shouts and curses followed the first shot fired, while more blossoms of orange opened in the night. Ed Miller saw a small figure dart across the background of muzzle flashes and fired. He heard a high-pitched cry and saw the shadowy image bowled over. Jubilant, he raised up and raced forward.

He took only three steps before he realized that someone else must be there, protecting the camp, or the boys had somehow obtained firearms. To left and right, Will and Vic worked actions of their repeating rifles smoothly, maintaining a steady rate of fire. Encouraged, he took another step and the world turned bright white for a fraction of a second before the utter darkness of eternity claimed him.

* * *

Rebecca nearly shouted when she saw the familiar shape of Joey rise and start to run around the fire ring to protect his friend, *Hoka*. A fleeting second later, she wished she had. *Oh, Joey, Joey,* she cried in silent anguish as the shot she heard fired was followed by the sudden pained cry and thump of a small boy. Anger overrode her uncertain grief and she took careful aim. A gentle squeeze and . . .

The beefy man in front of her grunted and staggered to one side. He raised his hands in supplication, though his body no long received messages from his shattered brain. Another uncoordinated step and he fell face first to the rough ground. To her right she heard another pained grunt and glanced that way in time to see Whirlwind bend double and collapse over his rifle. He had fallen close enough that she could go to his aid.

Crouching at his side, she heard a labored wheeze and muffled gurgle and knew, sinkingly, that the worst had come for Whirlwind. Tears stung her eyes. Her beloved son and her lover all in one brief battle with worthless scum. Rage seethed in her breast and she raised up to take in the two muzzle blasts of the remaining outlaws. Shouting out her fury, she advanced on them, Winchester held to her hip, hand stroking the lever action and squeezing off rounds until the weapon ran dry. Screaming her heartbreak, she let the rifle slip and drew a revolver from her waistband.

"Come out of there!" she challenged. "Fight me, you bastards."

Stinging pain bit into her shoulder and she reeled drunkenly. All the same, she managed to trigger two shots.

Will Hardesty couldn't believe it. His carefully laid attack on four helpless boys had turned into a nightmare. Who were these people? He hadn't time to consider the question his panicked mind raised. Shots came at them from everywhere. He saw Ed Miller rise up and start toward the fire ring. Saw him shoot one of the boys. Heard the anguished cry of a woman.

Then someone loosed the Furies of Hell.

Ed was blasted out of existence and the screaming woman came directly at him. He held his fire, fearful that the muzzle bloom would betray his exact position. It did little good. She seemed to know precisely where he stood. Hot lead cracked close by, shredding limbs and leaves of the trees, and still she came. At last her rifle ceased firing. Will breathed a deep sigh of relief.

Quickly he fired at her.

Then a sledge hammer smashed into his chest, followed by another terrible blow that numbed his body from the waist down. Staggered by the impacts, his body no longer obeying the frantic orders of his mind, he sagged to his knees. Gasping, he groped at the awful hurts in his body. His questing fingers told him too much. In utter anguish at the knowledge of his own mortality, Will Hardesty threw back his head and cried his last to an unhearing and uncaring diety.

"Oh, God, is this all?"

217

Terrible and potent silence fell over the tiny battle ground. The brush rustled and Victor Parks stepped into the open, hands over his head.

"Don't shoot. Don't kill me. I'm not armed."

"Come this way," a deep male voice commanded.

Lone Wolf found flint and steel and quickly kindled a new fire. Pale and shaken, their prisoner stood near him, under the guns of five Sioux, including Big Ears. In the light of the fresh blaze, Lone Wolf counted the ghastly toll.

Joey Ridgeway lay on one side, a bullet hole through the fleshy part of his side. He had bled a lot and his breath was shallow and irregular. Lone Wolf reckoned he would live. A short way away, Whirlwind lay still in death. Ten feet in front of him, Rebecca stirred feebly and tried to rise. She had been shot through the upper arm.

"Don't let it be the bone," Lone Wolf said aloud as he hurried to her side.

"Di—did I get him?" Rebecca asked shakily.

"Yes," Lone Wolf answered without knowing. "Let me see that arm."

A gentle probing of her left arm showed no indication of a broken bone. Lone Wolf thanked the Spirits. Pain filled Rebecca's eyes, not from her wound but an overwhelming grief.

"Whirlwind?" she asked breathily.

"He's dead, Becky. I'm sorry but he is."

Tears flooded Rebecca's cheeks. "And . . . Jo—Joe—Joey, too, then?"

"No," he told her, glad for this small bit.

"Take me to him," she pleaded as only a mother could.

"We have a prisoner . . ." Lone Wolf prompted.

"Kill him," her bitterness and grief dictated. "But first, take me to my son."

"You're lucky we didn't follow her instructions," Lone Wolf informed Vick Parks the next morning, a nod of his head indicating Rebecca. "She wanted us to hang you."

"Oh, my God," Parks gasped.

"As it is, I imagine the good people of the Army will have that pleasure. I'm taking you with me."

"What about them?" Parks pointed to the three mounted boys, a fourth on a travois, watched over carefully by Rebecca and Big Nose.

"They're going back to the Rosebud Agency," Lone Wolf said flatly. "I'm to join them after you're taken care of. She's been given more grief than any one person can handle in only a year. Be glad she also has a strong mind."

"I — I'd like to speak to her," Parks appealed.

"She won't talk to you. Until she's through mourning for Whirlwind, she won't talk to many people. That's enough of this. It's pointless," Lone Wolf cut off the conversation. He walked away from the prisoner and stopped beside the semi-conscious Joey and Rebecca.

"We're ready," he announced simply.

"Go, then," she replied in a dull, flat tone.

"You'll be all right?" her friend of many years and travails inquired with sincere sympathy.

"I . . . I'll never be all right again. Not — not like it used to be. Still, there will come a new day, when I

219

see the world in fresh colors and the sweet wind whispers to me that all is well again. Whirlwind taught me that, did you know?"

Silent, for there was nothing else to say, the old and dear friends parted.

BOLT IS A LOVER AND A FIGHTER!

BOLT
Zebra's Blockbuster Adult Western Series
by Cort Martin

ASHES
by William W. Johnstone

OUT OF THE ASHES (1137, $3.50)

Ben Raines hadn't looked forward to the War, but he knew it was coming. After the balloons went up, Ben was one of the survivors, fighting his way across the country, searching for his family, and leading a band of new pioneers attempting to bring American OUT OF THE ASHES.

FIRE IN THE ASHES (1310, $3.50)

It's 1999 and the world as we know it no longer exists. Ben Raines, leader of the Resistance, must regroup his rebels and prep them for bloody guerrilla war. But are they ready to face an even fiercer foe—the human mutants threatening to overpower the world!

ANARCHY IN THE ASHES (1387, $3.50)

Out of the smoldering nuclear wreckage of World War III, Ben Raines has emerged as the strong leader the Resistance needs. When Sam Hartline, the mercenary, joins forces with an invading army of Russians, Ben and his people raise a bloody banner of defiance to defend earth's last bastion of freedom.

SMOKE FROM THE ASHES (2191, $3.50)

Swarming across America's Southern tier march the avenging soldiers of Libyan blood terrorist Khamsin. Lurking in the blackened ruins of once-great cities are the mutant Night People, crazed killers of all who dare enter their domain. Only Ben Raines, his son Buddy, and a handful of Ben's Rebel Army remain to strike a blow for the survival of America and the future of the free world!

ALONE IN THE ASHES (1721, $3.50)

In this hellish new world there are human animals and Ben Raines—famed soldier and survival expert—soon becomes their hunted prey. He desperately tries to stay one step ahead of death, but no one can survive ALONE IN THE ASHES.

Available wherever paperbacks are sold, or order direct from the Publisher. Send cover price plus 50¢ per copy for mailing and handling to Zebra Books, Dept. 2315, 475 Park Avenue South, New York, N.Y. 10016. Residents of New York, New Jersey and Pennsylvania must include sales tax. DO NOT SEND CASH.